Also by Bill Thompson
From Indigo Sea Press

Celia Whitfield's Boy

Listen to the Southwind

indigoseapress.com

Chasing Jubal

By

Bill Thompson

Sepia Books
Published by Indigo Sea Press

Winston-Salem

Sepia Books
Indigo Sea Press
PO Box 67201
Winston-Salem, NC 27114

For information regarding bulk purchases of this book, digital
purchase and special discounts, please contact the publisher at
indigoseapress@gmail.com

Cover design by Bill Thompson
Cover Photo by Southwind Photography
Manufactured in the United States of America
ISBN 978-163066-462-6

Author's Note

There is nothing more real than the imagination of a fifteen-year-old boy. I spent a large portion of my working life at Boys and Girls Homes of North Carolina. Over the years I heard many boys tell me their stories. Some were so fanciful they couldn't possibly be true. Some were starkly real yet they challenged the boundary of credibility. But I realized in many cases the boys believed their stories even if they made them up. The wanted a story that would help them realize who they were because nobody else knew, nobody else was going to tell their story like they would and nobody knew them like they knew themselves. Sometimes their stories created questions that didn't have answers so they made up some. Sometimes they just chose to ignore the questions.

In *Chasing Jubal,* I wanted to tell a story like those boys told, a coming-of-age story full of fantasy and reality, a mixture so complex that it would be hard to separate the two. I wanted to tell about a boy who learns how to deal with life from the diverse people he meets- some real and some not real.

I set this story in a small southern town in the 1950s. That period of time was the last Age of Innocence for America. Those of us who grew up in that time would always look back on it as our formative years. We would form our opinions of the world and ourselves based on what went on around us during that period before we questioned the purpose of the Viet Nam war, faced ourselves during the civil rights movement and before technology would dominate our lives.

Life was simple then and optimistic and our imagination knew no bounds. This story is a reflection of that time.

Bill Thompson

Chapter 1

"The truth is too precious to waste. It oughta be measured out and used sparingly. Sometimes a good lie can serve well until the truth becomes an absolute necessity." That's what I said at Jubal Simpson's funeral. I attributed that bit of pseudo-wisdom to Jubal as the little church congregation gathered to memorialize a man who was a legend in the small town of Taggart, Virginia.

"Jubal was one of the most interesting people I ever met. Every day to him was another chance to do something different from what he had done the day before. He sure made my life interesting." I said some other things about my friend while I was standing up there, but it was more run-of-the-mill eulogy and didn't really say as much about Jubal.

Probably nobody else in town knew Jubal as well as I did. We had known each other our whole lives. We went to church and school together, prowled the streets of the town and explored the woods and fields that were all a part of life in that part of Virginia. My father, Raymond Lovejoy, Sr., owned the local newspaper and hired us to deliver the paper and then sell it on the street corner back when the paper was a daily publication. By the time I graduated from college and came home to take over the business, the newspaper was printed just twice a week. Jubal was still selling the paper from the newsstand in the lobby of The Cavalier Hotel when he died at seventy-five years old.

Jubal also owned The Cavalier Hotel.

As close as we were, our family backgrounds were very different. Jubal's father was killed during World War II toward the last part of the war. That made his mother a widow with two sons, Jubal and James McDonald Simpson III. Everybody called him Mac. He was just thirteen and Jubal was ten when their daddy died.

My dad ran the local newspaper and took care of me. My mother died when I was little; and Jubal's mom, who I called Miss Jane, was kind of a surrogate mother to me.

It was a sunny and clear but relatively cool day in early July of 1945 when Jane Simpson saw two men in Army uniforms come into Hanson's Hardware Store where she was the bookkeeper. When one of the soldiers asked Jake Hanson if Mrs. Simpson was in, she knew what they were there for. The whole town had just had a big Fourth of July celebration; but all that patriotic fervor seemed unimportant to Jane when the soldier told her that her husband had given his life for his country on an island called Okinawa, a place a long way from Taggart, Virginia.

So they brought Jim Simpson home and held a full military funeral with taps and everything and gave Jane an American flag folded into a neat triangle. Just about everybody in town brought food to the Simpson house. They offered their sympathy and condolences as best they knew how. But when they had left and the counters had been cleaned and the dishes washed, Jane cried and Jubal and Mac cried until there were no more tears; and then they took up their lives as best they could.

War has a way of unraveling dreams, of setting aside plans that had been made and forcing new ones. Those plans are seldom arrived at in a hurry or on purpose; more likely they just gather themselves together in a slow process over a period of time. At least, that was the way with the Simpson family. Miss Jane didn't see any reason to stop working at the hardware store or to do anything that she hadn't been already doing. She knew that she had to keep her family together so she kept on working, and the boys found little jobs after school and in the summer. They continued to live in the little house that Jim had built on Waverly Street; and when the Society for the Preservation of the Lost Cause asked about buying one of the two acres that the house sat on to build a meeting hall, she sold it to them. The money she got from the sale of that little lot meant that she owned the remaining house and lot free and clear. Her family would always have a place to live.

Mac and Jubal continued in school, made good grades. Mac was a good athlete, a stand-out baseball player and a serious student. Jubal was more fragile physically but never let that hold him back when it came to sports. He sat on the bench for football, basketball and baseball and enjoyed every minute of it. Jubal seemed to soak up life. He joyed in his brother's accomplishments and was quick to say, "That's my brother!" when Mac would bring the hometown crowd to its feet during a game.

Mac, in turn, was very protective of his younger brother. He encouraged him in everything he tried to do and was proud when Jubal shone in the stage productions at school. Jubal loved singing and acting. He liked being the center of attention. And his teachers and classmates encouraged him.

Mac had consciously assumed the role of man of the house after his father died, and Jubal almost idolized his brother.

'Course it would just be supposition to say that the lives of the members of the Simpson family would have pretty much reflected the lives of hundreds of other families who had lost men in the war if things hadn't happened like they did the day of Mac's high school graduation.

It started out like one of those days poets write about: a sky blue and soft like a baby blanket covering the earth, the sun creating just enough warmth to make a breeze feel good. The smell of gardenias in Jane's backyard evoked the memory of past ceremonies at church and school where the scent of the white flowers wafted across anxious families and friends seated row to row as an important rite transpired before them.

Just about the whole town gathered for graduation. There weren't a lot of occasions for celebration in Taggart so a graduation ceremony served as not just something families took part in but something the whole town shared. After all, everybody not only knew all the students who would be graduating but also probably had had some hand in their rearing. "It takes a village to raise a child" was an unspoken philosophy of the folks in Taggart long before it became a catch phrase for politicians and pseudosociologists.

The single dark cloud that formed to the west of town could have been an omen if anybody had wanted to see it that way. They could see it just over the top of the mountains as they arrived at the school auditorium. But nobody thought anything of it. Almost every summer day had a little shower late in the afternoon, and they'd all be inside by the time it got there anyway.

The auditorium was full; Jane and Jubal sat in the section reserved for families of the graduates. The warmth of the day had turned to heat and that, combined with the humidity and the crowded room, made the seat by an open window a lucky break for the Simpson family.

The Rev. T. Leonard Shipman from the First Baptist Church of Taggart gave the invocation. The glee club sang "Faith of our Fathers." The principal, Mr. Tom Callen, said a few words, then introduced Vernon Seymour, a 1921 graduate and president of the

Bank of Taggart who had recently donated the money for a new town library. As Mr. Seymour spoke, the wind picked up and the rain started. The first drops were big and singular like teardrops falling from the sky. Then it got heavy, the wind whipping it in sheets down from the mountains. The windows were too high for anybody to reach to close them so the wind was blowing the rain almost unimpeded into the auditorium. The slap of the old wooden seats caused a real distraction as everybody on the west side of the building rose and moved to the back and stood along the wall. The air had cooled some; but the dampness of the air in the building and on some of the audience seemed to intensify the faint smell of perfume and aftershave and genteel perspiration, particularly for those folks crowded together along the walls.

The rumble of thunder started about the same time Darlene McLure stood to give her salutatory address. The lights flickered and died, along with the sound system. Darlene was a smart girl and had written a great speech, but her voice couldn't compete with nature's din. However, she persevered and finished to polite applause.

Leroy Covington was the class valedictorian. As he approached the lectern to give his speech, a clap of thunder sounded so loudly that the building shook. In a good strong voice, he said, "I think the Lord is telling me to cut this short so in deference to my classmates and those of you who are already wet from the rain, I would ask Mr.

Callen if we could go ahead and award the diplomas and, if the storm quiets down, I'll be glad to give my speech then."

Following some appreciative applause, Mr. Callen declared that he appreciated Leroy's chivalry; and he proceeded to call all the names of the soon-to-be graduates. The ceremony was conducted as a solemn and dignified affair. The audience was silent as all eyes watched the students walk across stage. High school graduation was a significant achievement that warranted a respectful silence. As Mr. Callen shouted out the names, Mr. Clarence Dutton, chairman of the local school board, handed out the diplomas. Each one of the class superlatives was recognized when his or her name was called. Minnie Stevens was Best All-Around Girl mainly because at six-three she had led the girls' basketball team to the conference championship. When Mr. Callen said, "James McDonald Simpson III, Best All-Around Boy," Jubal shouted, "Yay, Mac!" Some folks laughed, some looked around to find the person who dared to break the somberness of the occasion and Jane Simpson flushed with embarrassment and pride.

After the last name had been read and all the students were standing back at their seats, Mr. Callen pronounced them all graduates; and they moved their tassels from the right side of their square-topped caps to the left. Since the storm had not abated, Leroy never got to give his speech. Reverend Shipman gave a quick benediction heard only by God due to the noise of the storm. Then

Miss Emoline Creech, the music teacher, played "Pomp and Circumstance" as the graduates marched out into the lobby of the auditorium to be joined by family and friends.

'Course, there wasn't room for everybody in the lobby, so some of the graduates worked their way back into the auditorium to mingle. Since Jubal and his mother had been standing at the back of the building, they were able to join Mac in the lobby. Miss Jane gave her older son a hug, and Jubal shook his hand. Jubal stood for a few minutes, both hands in his pants pockets, watching as folks came by to congratulate his brother. After a few minutes of feeling completely out of place, he walked over to the wide front door of the building. Some of the men had also gone there and were standing back away from the spray of the falling rain as it pounded the concrete steps that led up to the canopied doorway.

"Well, I believe the drought is over," joked one of the men. A hollow laughter followed as the men's faces looked seriously at the water now blowing across the dirt parking lot and the wind whipping the trees like pom-poms at a ball game. As they stared out the doorway, a deafening clap of thunder sounded, followed by a sizzling bolt of lightning that struck the pecan tree in the parking lot. The force of the bolt split the tree as a plume of smoke appeared and quickly disappeared, the infant fire squelched by the rain. Half of the tree fell to the ground and the other half across the top of a car that had probably been parked there to take advantage of the earlier shade.

"Time to go home, Molly," one of the men said solemnly to his wife. That declaration was the stimulus that got the whole crowd moving. Some women waited for their husbands to bring the cars to the front of the steps while others plunged into the rain and wind, unwilling to wait.

In a fairly short time, all the cars—except the one with the tree on it— were gone from the parking lot, and the only people left in the lobby were those who had walked to the ceremony. The Simpson family only lived a few blocks away so they had walked. They also walked because they didn't own a car. Money was tight, and they lived within walking distance of every place they needed to go.

Several people had offered them a ride home; but Jane had said, "Thank you" but they'd just wait out the storm.

Darius Clinton, the school janitor, was the only person still there as the three Simpsons stood in the lobby, the stormy darkness closing in. Darius had gone into the basement and found a ladder which he used to climb up and close the windows in the auditorium. After he had secured all the windows, he came into the lobby and looked out at the rain, then back at Jane. "Miss Jane, I gotta lock up now. I hate to run y'all out in this mess, but I got to git home and see how my family's doing."

"I don't blame you a bit, Darius," she responded. "I guess we'll just have to get wet. I don't believe this is going to slack up any time soon." So they stepped out in the rain, Jane holding Mac's arm and

Jubal walking quickly ahead, their heads bent against the pelting rain, their clothes already soaked after just a few steps.

Fortunately, the streets in that part of town had been paved; but the town of Taggart had not gotten around to adding any sidewalks or any drainage construction. As a result, the water was beginning to build up; and it ran across the tops of their shoes as the Simpsons hurried home. The street lights that had recently been put up gave some guidance as night overtook the soggy trio. Just as they turned the corner onto Waverly Street, they heard a thunderous prelude to another bolt of lightning that struck somewhere close by. The street lights went out, and they could see a power transformer spewing sparks just past their house.

They waded on through the water to the porch of their house. Just as Jane reached to open the front door, the black hearse pulled up. The driver rolled the window down and shouted, "Y'all come get in here! They say the river's run over its banks, and the whole town'll be under water by morning!"

Leon McCoy was the driver of the hearse. He ran The McCoy Funeral Home, and he used the hearse as an ambulance when needed for emergencies like wrecks on the highway or fires or, as in this case, floods. He had a flashing light that he could put on the top to indicate the status of the vehicle. That day the yellow light was in place.

The boys automatically looked at their mother for a response.

She said, "Y'all go get in the ambulance. I'll get some dry clothes and come on." Then she hollered to Leon, "We'll be right there." But the boys went into the house with their mother, and each of them quickly gathered up some clothes before running through the rain to the waiting hearse.

Jane sat in the front seat beside Leon as Mac and Jubal scrabbled into the back. She said, "We sure do appreciate you coming to get us, Leon. What in the world made you think of us?"

"Well, I saw y'all standing there at the school when I took Mama home and I remembered you didn't have a car, so when I heard about the flood, I thought I'd come and get you."

"That was very thoughtful of you, and I am so glad you did. I didn't realize we would be flooded. Gracious, we could have been swept away during the night if you hadn't come by."

Jubal and Mac, stretched out in the back of the hearse/ambulance, looked at each other with a grin. *Leon was no fool*, they thought. Mama was a pretty widow and what better way to impress her than to save the damsel in distress from a raging flood.

"The funeral home sets up on the side of the hill east of town, you know, so I thought y'all could stay there 'til things dry out some," said Leon as he drove resolutely through the storm.

"When's the last time you had dead people back here, Leon?" asked Jubal, not really wanting an answer but wanting to change Leon's focus. Leon didn't answer.

11

Chapter 2

Somehow the town miraculously avoided being flooded. In fact, there was never any further mention of the possibility of flooding.

The rain had stopped a few hours after Leon had "rescued" the Simpson family, and they were returned safe and sound to their home on Waverly Street the next morning.

But it was not the last time that Leon McCoy would be calling at the Simpson house. The Saturday night after the rescue, Jane accompanied Leon to the movie at the Colonial Theater. Instead of the hearse, he arrived in a black 1949 Cadillac, part of the funeral home fleet but less gothic. Leon had told Jane they were going to see *Father of the Bride;* but that show had already finished its run and was replaced by *Abbott and Costello Meet the Killer*, not the best movie for a first date, but Jane seemed to enjoy it anyway.

Jane thought about inviting Leon over for Sunday dinner but decided it was too soon for such a visit. As it turned out, that was a good decision since Mac chose that time to talk about his future plans.

"Mama," he said, "I been thinking about joining the Army. I talked to the recruiter, and he says that's good training for getting a job and 'sides there's not any real job possibility for me right now here in Taggart. Whatcha think?"

Jane Simpson was not a woman to rush into any real decision making without long consideration. Her decision to go with Leon to the movie was one of the few impulsive things she had ever done.

Certainly, her son's future was not something that could be determined during one Sunday dinner conversation. "That's something we'll have to think a lot about, son. Right off the bat, I can tell you I'm not too inclined to have my son go into something dangerous. 'Course I know the war's over, but the army is always going off somewhere where there's the chance you could get killed. I keep hearing about this Korea business, and I don't even know what it's all about; but I'll bet it'll come to no good."

Jubal said, "If I was you, Mac, I'd join the cavalry. I'd find out where John Wayne was, and that's where I'd go. You can't go wrong if you follow John Wayne."

Mac continued on, "But, Mama, we can't afford for me to go to college. Mr. Callen said he'd do everything he could to help me get into UVA, but he couldn't promise anything about financial aid. I thought about the Navy; but there's just something about being on a boat, being isolated, that I don't like. If I needed to, I could walk or run a long way if I'm on land; but I can't swim all that good." He could see that his attempt at levity was lost on his mother.

"I bet you could float good, Mac. And you can dog paddle for just about forever. Remember when me and Raymond stole your clothes down at the mill pond, and Susie Whitehurst and those other girls came down there. If you were ever gonna drown, that woulda been the time," said Jubal with a grin.

Jubal's attempts at humor failed to lighten the mood at the dinner table. Jane was remembering the wartime service of her husband, and no amount of peace-time optimism could cloud the pain of that remembrance. The anxious waiting for letters, the news on the radio of the fighting and the eventual arrival of the soldiers at her door were still too close. She had lost her husband to the military; she didn't want to take a chance on losing her son.

So for the next few weeks, Mac didn't mention joining the army. He kept reviewing the pamphlets he had gotten from the Army recruiter down at the post office, but he didn't even discuss it with Jubal. It was probably something or everything that went on at the Fourth of July celebration that helped Mac make up his mind, but more likely the deciding factor was that his daddy had been a soldier.

By almost any standard, the Fourth of July parade that year was small. It wasn't small from a lack of effort by the Chamber of Commerce folks. They had called everybody they could think of and had finally wound up with enough entries to justify the effort. Alex Granville, a wounded veteran of Iwo Jima, was the parade marshal and led the parade. He was followed by three members of the Hanson family dressed in colonial costumes. Mr. James Hanson played a flute, little Bobby played a snare drum way too big for him and James Allen, the oldest son, carried an American flag with forty-nine stars.

Everybody along the parade route either saluted the flag or put their hand over their heart as the Hanson family marched by. Some shed a tear. World War II was still a recent memory, and patriotism was an emotional concept.

Several businesses had floats with employees and their families on board. About every other entry was a convertible with a beauty queen representing just about every fresh fruit and vegetable festival anywhere close by and, of course, the reigning Miss Taggart who would go on to compete in the Miss Virginia Pageant.

The parade organizers had tried in vain to find a marching band; but since school was out, it was hard to get everybody back together. They were able to get a contingent from the local chapter of the VFW to march and play whatever instruments they had, and they did a great job.

The Taggart Fire Department's new fire truck was the next-to-last entry, followed by the Custis County Mounted Rescue Unit. What with all the noise of the fire truck and the crowd, the horses were a little overwrought, which justified their position as the last unit.

Right after the parade, everybody moved down to the city park for the picnic. It was a real community affair where tables of food, prepared by the local folks, were laid out row after row. The Blue Ridge Boys bluegrass band made the shade of a big oak tree their stage and played while everybody ate. Life was good in Taggart, and everybody seemed to be aware of that condition and felt themselves fortunate to be celebrating the national holiday.

Mac seemed in a pensive mood among all the gaiety. He had been thinking about where he would fit into his town if the college doors were closed to him. He couldn't see himself working at one of the saw mills or at the cotton mill over toward Martinsville. He somehow knew that if he were ever going to make it in the world, he would have to leave Taggart. There was nothing here to bind him.

He wouldn't really be leaving anything or anybody behind. He had dated a few girls through high school, but no serious relationship had ever developed; and he knew that wherever he went, he would always have his family.

After an appropriate length of time to give everybody a chance to finish eating, the mayor went over to the shade tree where the bluegrass band was playing and commandeered one of the microphones. He made a short (for him) speech about the importance of the celebration, then introduced Lt. Granville, the parade marshal. The veteran approached the microphone with some reluctance. He thanked everybody for the honor of being the parade marshal. He said he was proud to be a citizen of the United States and of Taggart, Virginia. Then he said something that really got to

Mac. The old soldier, clad in his army uniform, stood before his hometown folks and said, "Y'all probably know I didn't exactly volunteer to join the Army when the war started; but when I got drafted, I knew I oughta go on and do my duty. All during the war, I was only in one battle; and that's the one where I got hurt. I didn't ever think of myself as a patriot. Still don't. I didn't think a lot about all the political stuff the politicians and generals talked about. I just figured that if the Japs won, I'd never get back to Taggart. When I got shot up at Iwo Jima, I didn't think I would get back here. But

I'm here today, and I guess that was worth all the fightin' and gettin' shot."

'Course, there was a lot of applause from the crowd, and pretty soon everybody either settled in playing some games or sat around talking while the band played a little longer.

Then everybody went home.

The whole afternoon had a real effect on Mac, especially what the lieutenant said about fighting for his home. But the country wasn't at war right then, so that wasn't the biggest reason to join the Army. Mac thought about that and more than anything else, he thought how his leaving would affect his mother. After his father died, Mac had felt very protective of his mother. She never complained or seemed to want for anything, but he knew that he would not take the place of his father. Then along had come Leon McCoy, and Jane's life seemed to brighten up a little. Mac didn't think Leon was anywhere near the man his daddy was; but if he made his mama happy, he was alright with Mac. Jubal and Mac had sorta come to an understanding that sooner or later their mother and Leon would get married, probably after Jubal graduated from high school.

The Army recruiter had told Mac about the advantages of the training he would receive if he joined up, something he could use after he got out. The Army would pay for him to go to Fort Bragg down in North Carolina to be examined, and then he'd be sent on to basic training. He thought that was what he'd go ahead and do. So that night he wrote one note to his mother, explaining how he felt and where he was going and another note to Jubal, telling him to take care of their mama. Then he caught the 11:30 a.m. bus to Greensboro where he would board another bus to Fayetteville and Fort Bragg.

Chapter 3

Jubal Simpson never did anything slowly, not even thinking. As soon as he saw the note on Mac's bed, he knew what had happened.

He quickly read his brother's instruction as to their mother's welfare. He thought only a minute before he took a sheet of notebook paper and wrote another note addressed to himself. He then set out with the note in hand for the Lovejoy house to find me.

Like most people in Taggart, we hardly ever locked our doors unless there was some notice that there had been an escape from the local prison or something equally catastrophic. So when Jubal got to the back door of the house, he didn't even slow down. He just pushed the door open and ran to my room. It was too early for anybody to be up, particularly on a Sunday morning. None of the businesses in town were open on Sunday; and Sunday school didn't start at any of the churches until 10 a.m., giving folks a few more minutes of sleep.

Jubal pulled back the bed cover from me and in a shouted whisper said, "Come on, Raymond, Mac's been kidnapped and we gotta go find him!"

"Kidnapped? What are you talking about? Why would anybody kidnap Mac?" was my sleepy response.

"Look. Here's the ransom note. It says 'Jubal I have been kidnaped (sic) by the army. Come and get me. Mac.' See? We gotta go get him!"

I quickly grabbed the note from Jubal's hand and looked at it. "This is not a ransom note. It's plain as day you wrote it. Now, what ails you?"

"Well, he coulda been kidnapped. You don't know. I mighta got a mental telephonic message that told me to write that note. Brothers can do that, you know, read each other's mind and stuff. He could be held in bondage and gonna be shipped off on some ship like being shanghaied by pirates, except it's the army. We gotta go get him! Come on!"

"Now, wait a minute, just wait a minute. You know as well as I do that Mac has not been kidnapped or shanghaied or any of that stuff. You know he's been talking about joining the Army almost since he graduated. I'm pretty sure that's what he's done. I heard him talk to the recruiter. It's my guess that Mac has enlisted and has gone to be examined down to Fort Bragg just like the recruiter told him."

"I just can't believe he'd decide to do something like that without telling me before he done it. He's my brother." That statement seemed to say it all for Jubal. Right then he didn't just miss his brother; he felt a little betrayed. "We do 'bout everything together, me and Mac do. He wouldn't just run off like that." The look on Jubal's face was a mixture of sad disbelief and puzzlement. He didn't want to think his brother could have reached that point in his life that would necessitate moving beyond the familiar boundaries of Taggart, that Mac would not always be there to give him advice about everything, to shield him, protect him and, most of all, give him that incomparable assurance that he had family. You can always depend on family.

He suddenly felt alone for the first time in his life. Although his mother was still the biggest and most irreplaceable part of his family, he had already realized that he was probably going to have to share her with Leon McCoy. Now he was going to have to share Mac with the Army.

Or maybe he would share the Army with Mac. What if he could go in the Army with Mac? He had heard about brothers doing that during The War Between the States. His Grandpa Loonis had told him about his father— Jubal's great-grandfather—and his brother joining General Early's army and staying together through the whole war. It was his Grandpa Loonis that had convinced his daughter to name her second-born son after the famous general. Jubal's thoughts solidified somewhat. He would join Mac, and they would both be soldiers together and share adventures like their ancestors. That was the answer to his dilemma.

Jubal looked over at me, the bedcovers still hanging on to me and said, "Whereabouts is Ft. Bragg?"

"It's down in North Carolina," I replied. "Kinda in the eastern part."

"The far east or the near east?"

"'Bout southeast, I reckon. Close to Fayetteville."

"Is it a long way?"

"Near 'bout 200 miles probably."

"That's where I'm going," said Jubal as he walked out of my bedroom.

"Hey, you can't just go to Ft. Bragg!" I shouted as I stood in my underwear, clutching the bed sheet and watching Jubal run out of the house and into the bright Sunday morning.

Jubal didn't really have a plan when he left my house, but he was working on one. First, he had to go back home and get a few things to take with him and somehow let his mama know where he was going without her being able to stop him. Jubal always thought in spurts with the hope that everything would fall in place once the ball got rolling.

It was quiet when he got back to his house. He figured his mother was still asleep, but he wouldn't have very long to get his stuff together and get on the road to Ft. Bragg.

The first thing he did when he got to his room was pull out that yellow legal pad on the little study desk and write his mother a note. "Mama. I need to respond to the call of destiny. Just as Greatgrandpa Rupert and Uncle Henry answered the call of Jubal Early to join the

Confederate army, so have I decided to follow my brother into the army. It is a call that cannot be denied any more than our father could deny his call either. We are a family of soldiers. Don't worry about us. We will come back just like Grandpa Rupert and Uncle Henry did." Jubal thought that struck just the right patriotic tone to keep his mama from worrying about him. Then he remembered that patriotism didn't keep her from worrying about his dad and look what happened to him. So he crumpled up that note and threw it in the trash can.

On a clean sheet of paper, he wrote, "Mama. Have gone with Mac. Love, Jubal." The closing was more of a plea than just a statement of his own affection.

The morning sun was just unwrapping the cool air from the night, the dew still heavy enough to wet the toes of Jubal's cloth sneakers. He had still not worked out a plan as to how he was going to get to Ft. Bragg. He did know that he had to go south, which meant across the Virginia line toward Greensboro, then follow the right road to Fayetteville. He had been to Greensboro once before but didn't remember much about it.

He walked quickly through the streets of dormant Taggart, hoping no one would see him. When he got to the railroad tracks that bisected the town, he decided to follow them out to the highway that headed south. After he passed the old fertilizer plant, he jumped the ditch that separated the railroad from the highway, one foot sinking into the wet ditch bank as he landed on the opposite side, leaving a muddy seal around one shoe. He stomped his feet on the solid highway pavement to shake the mud off, then continued walking. He felt like he was finally really on his way.

Since it was a Sunday morning, there was very little traffic on the highway. Jubal saw the lack of traffic as a two-edged sword. He figured that since so many people knew him, if they saw him walking away from town on Sunday morning, they'd know something was up since he was not headed to church. They'd probably stop and offer him a ride or even ask where he was headed.

That's just the way people were in Taggart. On the other hand, if he got lucky, somebody heading out of town might offer him a ride going toward Greensboro; and he could put a lot of distance between him and folks who would recognize him.

As he walked along the side of the road that morning, the sun shining on the left side of his face, he looked for something that would remind him of that previous trip; but it was such a vague memory that nothing looked familiar. The only thing he knew for sure was he needed to keep heading south. That meant keeping the sun to his left until afternoon.

Fortunately, the highway was mostly downhill with an occasional rise. As the morning wore on, Jubal began to walk a little slower; and when the highway curved sharply to the right where another paved road led to the left and down a hill, Jubal turned left.

24

After all, he needed to keep going south and it would be easier going downhill. He was surprised when he saw the road sign pointing back in the direction from which he had come. It read: "Taggart 5." The sun was almost straight overhead, and he had only walked five miles.

As Jubal continued down the small, unmarked paved road, he realized that in his haste to leave, he had only packed some clean underwear, a pair of jeans, a couple of shirts, a light jacket and some soap. No food and no water. And less than five dollars in his pocket. He was hungry and thirsty and already tired. The thought crossed his mind that maybe this idea of catching up with Mac was a little hasty; maybe he should have done some more planning. He thought about turning back but quickly dismissed the thought. It would take him the rest of the day to get back; he'd still be hungry and thirsty and even more tired, his mama would be mad at him and keep a closer watch on him and he'd still be in Taggart without his brother. So he kept on walking.

After about an hour without any traffic and not even the sign of a house, Jubal began to wonder if he were going the right way. As the noon hour passed, he remembered to keep the sun on his right to keep walking in a southern direction. 'Course, the road didn't always go south. In fact, it was getting more and more curvy as the hill got steeper and steeper. Jubal was having to watch his balance and brace himself, his feet sliding sometimes on the rocks beside the pavement. He watched the way before him as the pavement abruptly ended and the dusty, dirt road continued its precarious descent down the mountain.

Little dust devils swirled before him as the afternoon heat bore down. It had been a good while since Jubal had heard a sound other than the occasional tweet of a bird and the padding of his own feet. The stillness and the heat, the monotony of the dusty trek and a sense of dislocation began to slowly drain the optimism from Jubal's mind and the energy from his body. His thin cotton shirt was wet with perspiration, and his little suitcase had taken on the weight of a steamer trunk.

The relatively good news was that the road had leveled out some; the steep decline had become less sharp, almost undulating like a dusty brown tarpaulin waving in the summer sun.

Jubal's imagination began to seek some relief. This road before him wasn't a mountain in southwestern Virginia. It was a lonely desert out west where he was struggling to get back to the ranch. His horse had jumped at a rattlesnake, throwing Jubal to the ground before running off with his canteen of water and his rifle. He had to get back to the ranch to warn them that the Indians were planning to attack. Just ahead he could see a mustang standing by a muddy pool of water that was seeping from a hole pawed in the desert floor. The horse's head was held high, the desert wind blowing his long mane and tail. He heard the stallion whicker, beckoning him to share the precious water.

What he really heard was the bleating of a goat standing in a tall cornfield just a few feet from the Virginia road. He really didn't look much like a stallion; but he was standing with his head up, his tongue hanging out. He was a big goat, about as big as Jubal had ever seen. His black- and-white spotted coat was shiny and slick, and his tail wagged slowly.

Jubal thought that the presence of a goat meant there was a house, maybe a farm, close by where he could get a drink of water and rest a little while. But all he could see was a big cornfield, the summer stalks so tall he couldn't see anything else. For just a minute Jubal and the goat looked at each other. Jubal took a step toward the goat; and the goat turned slowly, took a few steps, then turned back continuing to wag his tail as he looked at Jubal.

It was apparent to Jubal that the goat wasn't going to lead him anywhere, not to a farm or even to a pool of muddy water. So Jubal continued his journey down the dirt road. For whatever reason, the goat followed him, keeping about thirty feet behind. If Jubal stopped, so did the goat. If he advanced toward the goat, the goat retreated. Seeing nothing to be gained by continuing to try to connect with the goat, Jubal proceeded with the goat following behind.

As the afternoon wore on, a soft, cool breeze began to blow down the road, ruffling the leaves of the cornstalks and bringing some relief to Jubal. And the goat. But the breeze didn't help the growl in Jubal's stomach or relieve his aching legs as the miles stretched into more miles without any sign of a farmstead or even a barn.

Jubal had not planned on his trip to catch up with Mac becoming a test of his survival skills. Generally speaking, he was not an outdoorsman. He had once joined the Boy Scout troop in Taggart but never got past the Tenderfoot level before the troop disbanded when the scoutmaster's company transferred him to the home office in Richmond. When the Methodist church revived the troop, Jubal decided to pass on that opportunity. He'd rather just read about adventure.

Just as the daylight began to fade, Jubal heard the sound of an automobile behind him. Excitedly he turned in the middle of the road and looked for his possible savior. As the sound of the engine got louder, Jubal saw the headlights of the vehicle come around a curve. He continued to stand in the middle of the road, not willing to take a chance that the driver might not see him if he stood on the side.

Suddenly he saw the goat silhouetted in the headlights between him and the approaching vehicle. Instinctively he ran toward the goat and the headlights in an effort to keep the goat from being slammed by the vehicle. There was the sound of tires sliding on the dirt road as the driver saw the goat and Jubal in front of him and applied the brakes. The confused goat didn't move. At the same instant that Jubal caught the goat, the vehicle came to a stop. Immediately a boy somewhat older than Jubal got out and shouted, "What the hell are you doing, boy? I coulda killed you and the damn goat!"

The headlights shone through the swirling dust on Jubal as he knelt on the ground with his arms wrapped around the goat. The driver stood in front of one of the headlights, casting a shadow that ended just short of the two in the middle of the road.

Jubal didn't answer. He was too tired and dusty and hot and relieved to make a reply. He knelt there with the goat in his arms until the boy came over and took the goat and put him in the back of the truck. "Come on," said the boy as he helped Jubal to his feet and walked him back to the truck. Jubal got in the cab of the truck without saying a word. The boy put the truck in gear and continued down the road. Abruptly he stopped the truck and got out, returning with Jubal's small suitcase which he placed in the back of the truck. "I guess that's your suitcase. Where you headed?"

"Thank you," Jubal said stoically as if he had been just hitching a ride. "I appreciate you coming by. I'm going to meet my brother at Ft. Bragg."

The driver looked over at the boy beside him. "Ft. Bragg's a long way from here. You planning on walking all the way?"

"Nope. I figured on catching rides with folks just like I did with

29

you. Didn't think the rides'd be so far apart though."

"You had anything to eat?"

"Nope. I left in kind of a hurry. Ain't even had breakfast. I could eat a mouthful if you happen to have any to spare."

"Left in a hurry, huh? You running away?"

"Not exactly. Just didn't ask anybody if I could go. Left Mama a note."

"I'll get you something to eat. I live just up here a little ways with my pa. He's probably got something set out for supper.

Probably not much, but it'll keep your belly button from rubbing against your backbone. Name's Billy Branson, by the way. What's yours?"

"Jubal Simpson."

That was the end of the conversation. The two rode along in silence, bouncing as the truck rattled over the washboard rutted road, the smell of dew-blended dust settling close behind them, the dim headlights slanting through the summer night.

The road ran along past rows of tall corn on the right side and a thick stand of pine trees on the other. No buildings—barns or houses—broke the monotony until Jubal saw a mailbox standing at the end of a narrow road that led to the left through the pines. Billy slowed the truck before making the turn on to the road and shifted into second gear. It was a road with two ruts divided by weeds so tall that the beating of the weeds and an occasional small bush striking the front and underside of the truck almost drowned out the sound of the engine. Occasionally Billy would slow the truck to a crawl as they passed through big mud holes, and Jubal could hear the water splashing away from the wheels and smell the sour odor of the mud.

Jubal was apprehensive. People who lived at the end of a road like this evidently didn't have much company and didn't get out much themselves. Where was he going? What kind of people lived in such isolation? He briefly considered jumping out of the truck; but, even as slow as it was going, he knew that wasn't possible. He sat up on the edge of the seat, looking anxiously ahead as he gripped the door handle.

Shortly he saw a spark of light in the distance beyond the headlights. It was a dim light, just a glimmer so faint he wasn't sure it was really there. As they got closer, the light became clearer but no brighter. When the road took a sharp turn to the right, he could see that the light was a lantern hanging on the porch of a small house. He couldn't tell much about the house in the dark, but he could tell it was unpainted and the lantern was hanging on a porch. The house sat in the midst of the pine trees. There was no yard, just a wide place in front of the porch steps where Billy stopped the truck.

Almost as soon as the truck stopped, a man opened the screen door and stood on the porch looking out toward the arrivals. "Where you been, boy? I was starting to worry about you," came the voice from the porch.

"Nowhere extra, Pa. Just picked me up a stray feller on the way back from Miss Caroline's prayer meeting. 'Bout run over him and his goat," Billy answered as he opened the truck door and walked around to Jubal's side of the truck. "Come on, Jubal. Want you to meet my pa."

Billy opened the truck door. Jubal didn't move. "It's alright, Jubal. He's my pa. He'll get us a bite to eat, and you can take your rest. Ain't nobody going to hurt you."

Jubal reluctantly stepped out of the truck. Billy put his arm around the boy's shoulders as they walked into the light from the porch. "This is Jubal Simpson, Pa. Jubal, this is my pa, the Reverend Josiah Branson."

The man on the porch was a short, balding man with a wispy grey beard that circled his face like moss on a cypress stump. He wore black pants held up by broad black suspenders over a longsleeved white shirt buttoned at the collar even in the summer heat.

With a smile, he said, "Well, hello, Jubal Simpson. Welcome to our home, humble as it is. You look like you could use a little food and maybe some soap and water. We've got a little of both that we'll be glad to share." He reached out his small, pudgy hand to Jubal who shook it unenthusiastically. The preacher chuckled, "Now, where is the goat?"

"In the back of the truck, Pa. He's not any worse for wear, but he probably ain't too happy after being bounced along that road and dusted pretty good."

The preacher released Jubal's hand and walked over and looked in the back of the truck. As he peered through the slats and the darkness trying to the see the goat, the animal bleated just as the preacher squinted between them. He jumped back and laughed. "I expect he ought to stay right there tonight, Billy. You can take him some water and a little food. We'll look after him some more in the morning."

As he walked back up on the porch, he opened the screen door and said, "Come on in, Jubal. Billy said he picked up a stray. You can tell me what you've strayed from while I fix us all something to eat."

The inside of the Branson house pretty much matched the outside. There were only three rooms: a kitchen /sitting area and two bedrooms. The kitchen was dimly lit by a large kerosene lantern hanging from the ceiling. There was a small fire in the woodburning cook stove to which the preacher added a couple sticks of wood from a box beside the stove.

"We don't eat fancy, Jubal, but we eat regularly; and the Lord provides for our needs. With His help we've been able to do without a lot of the things most folks would consider necessities, but we have found the lack of those things to be really fewer burdens." He picked up a glass pitcher filled with milk and poured some into a glass which he handed to Jubal. "Take that milk right there. It was still in the cow this morning; and we've got a hand-dug well that yields the coolest, clearest water you can find anywhere. We've got a garden that provides vegetables, some hogs that we butcher in the winter and a smokehouse to cure the hams. We've got wood to cook with and keep us warm in the winter and the cool breezes that blow down from the mountains to cool us in the summer. And we get along very well with the help of folks who feel led to support our ministry with a few monetary donations from time to time."

"Where's your church?" asked Jubal.

"Our ministry is to God's church, the people. You know, you don't have to have a building to have a church. A church is the people, God's children who gather together anywhere to worship. I merely go out among them along the highways and byways, on the streets and in the alleys, in the big cities and small towns and in the countryside, the forgotten and unseen places that society has ignored."

Jubal could see that the preacher was beginning to get wrought up about his preaching even as he took a pot off the stove and spooned out some butter beans and corn onto a plate and added a slice of salted pork before he placed it before Jubal. The preacher handed a large spoon to Jubal, then fixed another plate which he placed on the table in anticipation of Billy's arrival in the kitchen.

Despite the evangelical prelude to the meal, Jubal began to relax. The preacher seemed kind enough, if a little bit condescending as far as Jubal was concerned. Jubal thought he was acting like he was one of those "lost sheep" Reverend Jackson talked about back at the Baptist church in Taggart. In fact, Jubal had been going to church, to Sunday school and preaching every Sunday since he could remember. He was a member of the RAs (Royal Ambassadors, a boys' church group) and was a member of the Sword Drill Team in his Training Union class. He could find any verse in the Bible in about five seconds.

Billy came in and immediately sat down at the table and began to eat. "Shouldn't we ask the blessing, preacher?" asked Jubal.

"Oh, no. That's not necessary. I blessed it as I cooked it on that stove there. In fact, I have blessed every item in this house," responded the preacher.

"You mean you asked God to bless it," said Jubal.

"No," said the preacher. "Once God has given it to me, it is mine and I can further consecrate it with my blessing on it."

That was Jubal's first hint that the Reverend Josiah Branson was no ordinary preacher.

Chapter 4

I had just gotten dressed and was combing my hair when I heard the phone out in the hall ring. I figured it would be for Dad so I just let it ring. When it quit ringing and started ringing again right away, I figured Dad was already walking to church so I answered the phone.

"Raymond, is Jubal over there with you?" Miss Jane shouted into the phone.

"No, ma'am," I answered as calmly as I could. I should have known I'd be getting that call. Miss Jane always called over to my house any time she was looking for Jubal. Usually he was here.

"Well, where is he? If you two are up to some of your shenanigans, we're going to have a talk. This thing of leaving me some crazy note and expecting me to just go on like nothing's happened is just not something I'm going to put up with. Y'all shouldn't be playing around on a Sunday morning anyway. You'd think you could give the Lord at least one day out of the week without causing your families so much trouble and strife. Now, you tell him to get his butt back home and get ready for church, or he will be in serious trouble."

I didn't know what to do. Jubal was my best friend, and I didn't want to get him in trouble; but there was something in Miss Jane's voice that told me she was worried way beyond her usual agitation with me and Jubal. I didn't want to get her any more upset so I told her, "Well, he did come by here earlier this morning and said something about going to see Mac. Wanted me to go with him, but you know me, Miss Jane, I wanted to keep the Sabbath holy; and I tried to talk him out of going on a Sunday but...."

"Raymond Lovejoy, don't give me any of your usual mess. If Jubal's run off somewhere, I need to find him; and I don't need you beating around the bush if you know where he is."

Her original anger was gone, and she was now pleading with me to help her. I said, "Yes, ma'am. He did come by here, and he first tried to tell me Mac had been kidnapped by pirates or something like that and wanted me to help go rescue him, but I knew there wasn't any kidnapping...."

"Raymond, don't play with me! Where is Jubal?"

"I'm trying to tell you, Miss Jane. I really don't know where he is. All I know is he said he was going to be a soldier with Mac and that he was headed to Fort Bragg."

"Alright, Raymond. You get your daddy and y'all come to my house right now. I'm going to call Leon and then I'm going to call the sheriff, and we are going to find Jubal." And she hung up the phone.

Miss Jane Simpson was a lady, a genteel Southern lady who

believed in doing everything in a certain way, a manner handed down through generations of genteel Southern ladies. Her way of doing things went far beyond the usual ideas of etiquette and formal social interaction. She believed that everyone had the right to express their opinions and to conduct their affairs in whatever manner suited them as long as it wasn't offensive to others. What was offensive followed a very detailed definition that had evolved in her own mind growing up in a small Southern town where one individual's action affected almost every other individual.

Essentially, you didn't do anything to upset your neighbors. Good people always did the proper thing. Though most often she accomplished her goals with a subtlety that belied her earnestness, sometimes when she felt that the end justified the means, she forsook propriety and engaged in the more direct approach. Her search for Jubal was one of those occasions.

When I went to the church to find my father and relay Miss Jane's instruction, he didn't hesitate. He didn't even excuse himself; he just got his hat from the shelf in the back of the men's Sunday school classroom and walked immediately the two blocks to the Simpsons' residence. I filled him in on Jubal's escapade as we walked. Leon McKoy was already there, as evidenced by the hearse parked at an angle in front of the house.

"Come on in, Ray," Miss Jane instructed when she heard us step on the porch. Even before the door closed behind us, Miss Jane said,

"Y'all have a seat over there on the sofa. Give me your hat, Ray."

Daddy and I sat beside Leon on the sofa. We all sat on the edge of the seat, our feet flat on the floor as we awaited Miss Jane's direction.

"I want y'all to get Jubal back here right away. We will do whatever is necessary to make that happen. Ray, you are a member of the town council so I want you to get the police chief to send out a notice that Jubal is missing. I want him to send that notice to every county in North Carolina. I know Jubal said he was going to Fort Bragg; but he doesn't even know where that is, and his sense of direction is whimsical at best. I also think you ought to send out some kind of news story to all the newspapers on teletype or mail or whatever is the best way to spread the word.

"Leon, I want you and Raymond to go right now and look for him. There are only so many roads leading south and in the general direction of Fort Bragg. You drive down those roads and ask people if they have seen a forlorn boy wandering that way. Stop and call me every four hours." ("Forlorn" was Miss Jane's opinion of Jubal's appearance, which had no basis in fact.)

My daddy was a man who was used to giving orders, not following them; but he never said a word during that brief meeting with Miss Jane. We all got up from the sofa and proceeded to follow our instructions. I went back to the house and packed a few items to take on what I hoped was a short trip. Leon picked me up in the hearse a few minutes later.

Daddy went straight to the police station and told Chief Gains what Miss Jane said, then went to the newspaper office where he wrote an article that he sent directly to the Associated Press wire service. He didn't even remember he had left his hat at Miss Jane's until the next day.

Miss Jane's sense of urgency must have been contagious because Leon had the red light on the hearse going when he picked me up. He sped down the narrow streets of Taggart as if he were rushing to a wreck out on the highway. He didn't say a word until we got to the divide in the highway just past the fertilizer plant when he asked, "Which way?" and stopped the car in the middle of the road.

As I look back at that particular inquiry, I realized that it was more than just a question; it was a recognition of our situation. We had no idea what we were doing. We had reacted to Miss Jane's dominating personality and overwhelming sense of loss and urgency without even thinking about the implications of what she was telling us to do. We didn't even have a road map.

We sat there in silence, trying to figure out our next move.

Finally I said, "Alright, let's try to think like Jubal. All he knows about getting to Fort Bragg is that it's south of here. We learned in Boy Scouts that if we are lost, we head north, which means the sun would be on our right in the morning and on our left in the afternoon, so south right now is directly in front of us. Or was it the other way around?"

"Well, the sun comes up in the east every morning so that's on our left right now so if we gonna follow your reasoning, we just keep on going the way we're going if we wanna go south," reasoned Leon.

So, we headed south—or at least as far as we knew, we headed south—in pursuit of Jubal, who may or may not have been headed in the same direction.

Leon McCoy drove the hearse like it was an ambulance. He didn't have a flashing light going, but otherwise he was proceeding down the road in much the same way he would have if we had been responding to a car wreck. We didn't know where we were going, but we were making good time getting there.

I didn't know Leon very well. I had seen him around town at various functions, particularly, of course, at funerals. He went to the same church as my family did, but I had not seen him there very often until he started calling on Miss Jane. He was the epitome of ordinary-looking: average height, average weight, not very tall, not very short. About the only thing that was distinctive about Leon was the fact that he always wore a suit and tie. Even in the summer when all the other men in town, including my father, would forego such attire in the sweltering heat, Leon wore a coat and tie. The one waiver from his sartorial routine was sometimes he would wear a blue shirt instead of a white one.

He had not spoken since we started our search for Jubal, except that one inquiry as in what direction we should proceed. Otherwise he was focused on the road ahead, both hands on the steering wheel.

Chapter 5

Jubal had no problem falling asleep on the pallet Billy placed on the floor in his bedroom and awoke feeling anxious to be back on his journey to join Mac. The smell of bacon and eggs pulled him into the kitchen where the preacher had already set the food on the table.

"Sun's been up a good while now. I was beginning to think the Devil of Darkness had swept you away from us. Go ahead and sit and eat. Billy's gone to milk the cow and check on your goat. He'll be back directly."

Rev. Branson placed food at the three places at the table, then sat down and began to eat with Jubal. Billy came in and wordlessly joined in eating the meal. No one spoke until Billy said, "I got everything loaded on the big truck, Pa. We can leave anytime. We taking Jubal with us?"

"Certainly Jubal is welcome to go with us." He then turned to Jubal and asked, "Would you like to accompany Billy and me on our crusade?"

"Where you going?" asked Jubal.

"To do God's work," replied the preacher.

"What I mean is what direction are you going? I'm still going

43

to Fort Bragg to get up with my brother. If you're heading in that direction, I'd be pleased to ride along."

"We have no specific destination," replied the preacher. "We go wherever the Lord calls us. You, my boy, could be God's messenger telling us to go south toward Fort Bragg."

"Oh, I'm not carrying any message. I'm just telling you I'm going to Fort Bragg; and if you're going that way, I'd appreciate the ride."

"Fort Bragg it is!" declared Rev. Branson as he stood and began to gather the dishes from the table even as Billy and Jubal rushed to eat the food still on the plates. "Time and the Devil wait for no man."

As the old man cleaned up the kitchen, Billy and Jubal gathered their respective suitcases and took them outside. Jubal had not seen the big truck the night before. It was an old truck like Mr. Hardiman had down at his furniture store in Taggart. The bed of the truck was completely enclosed and had a portion of the storage area over the cab of the truck. On the side painted in red were the words, "Branson Evangelistic Crusade."

"Good job of letterin', ain't it?" asked Billy as they put their suitcases behind the seat in the cab of the truck. "Cost a pretty penny to get a real sign painter in Danville to put that on there. 'Course we could only afford to put it on one side. I coulda done it myself, but Pa said we needed to make a good first impression when we drove into towns. Mine might not a-been as pretty, but it woulda been a good imitation; and we coulda put it on both sides."

Rev. Branson came out of the house and almost trotted to the truck. "Come on, boys. If we hurry, we can spread the light of the gospel before the racing shadow of sin overtakes another sinner."

With that challenge before them, Billy aimed the truck down the dusty road toward an unknown destination.

Jubal was wedged between the preacher and Billy in the cab of the truck as they bounced along the narrow dirt road. The preacher had leaned his head against the back of the seat and was fast asleep. The windows were rolled down, but even the wind blowing in was hot and every time they stopped at a stop sign, dust fogged in. Fortunately, after about an hour of such travel, the dirt road changed to a narrow, two-lane asphalt highway; and a certain amount of comfort settled into the cab of the truck.

Jubal was forced to sit with his legs on the right side of the gear shift rising from the floor of the cab. Because the road through the hills of the Virginia countryside were often steep, Billy had to shift the gears to climb and sometimes slow down the speed of the truck going downhill. "You gotta downshift on some of these hills," Billy said. "Just putting on the brakes ain't gonna cut it. Lotta weight back there. Wear out the brakes, then where'd you be?"

"How'd you learn to drive a truck?" asked Jubal.

"From a feller used to travel with us. He got saved one night at one of Pa's revivals and said that God told him to drive this truck.

He taught me how to drive; then, when he left, I took over."

"What happened to the man?"

"Pa said the devil took him back, but I believe it was that woman in Martinsville that took him. They kinda got together when she played the piano for a service there, then him and her left after the service the next night. I'm glad the devil let him go long enough to teach me to drive this truck. When Pa drives it, he gets to thinking about spiritual stuff; and before you know it, we in a ditch or running somebody off the road. Pa says I'm an anointed driver."

Sometime about the middle of the day, the evangelistic trio pulled off the road and parked in an open field next to a country store. "J.C. Devlin's Store" was written on a long, narrow CocaCola sign attached to two posts that supported the roof of the front porch of the store.

"Come on, boys, it's time for our mid-day meal," declared the preacher as they exited the old truck and walked toward the store. The noontime heat swept down on them like a blanket. A few spots of rust had worked into the Esso sign hanging over a single gasoline pump rising from the dirt a few feet from the porch. The tin roof of the building sent off shimmering waves of heat even as it shaded the man sitting in the rocking chair on the porch. The man's bulky body was clothed in the uniform of a country storekeeper: short-sleeve khaki shirt tucked into khaki pants held up by wide, black suspenders with white socks and black, crepe-soled shoes. As the travelers stepped up on the porch steps, the storekeeper picked up a number-ten peach can and spat a large dollop of tobacco juice into it.

"Hot as hell, ain't it?" said the storekeeper, making it more of a statement than a question.

"Not having ever actually been to hell, I can't attest to the veracity of the analogy; but I would venture to say that this earthly heat is merely warm, compared to the eternal blast of the Devil's hearth," replied the reverend. "However that may be, it is the discomfort of travel combined with the passion of the sun that causes us to seek some solace in your establishment in the form of food and drink and a shady respite."

The storekeeper shifted his wad of tobacco to the other side of his mouth and his weight to the front of the chair. He bent forward, placing his elbow on one arm of the chair and the palm of his hand on the other, his face expressionless as he stared in silence at the preacher. "Okay," he said as he stood up with some effort, opened the screen door and walked into the store. The travelers followed him.

A large electric fan stood on a steel pedestal at the back of the store. The fan moved slowly from side to side, blowing the collective smell of clothing, leather, animal feed and kerosene toward the front of the store. Ceiling-high shelves of canned food rose behind the counter where the storekeeper stood. A ladder on wheels waited at the end of the shelves to assist in the acquisition of the items placed there.

"We'll have a can of those sardines there, a can of Vienna sausages, a small box of saltine crackers, a slice of that hoop cheese and three bottles of Coca-Cola," instructed Mr. Branson.

The storekeeper fetched the items, placed them beside the cash register, spat tobacco juice into a can under the counter and said, "That'll be seventy-five cents."

The preacher handed him a dollar bill and said, "Keep the change as a token of our appreciation for your assistance in our hour of need."

Wordlessly the storekeeper punched the keys of the cash register, pulled the handle on the side and, as a small bell rang, deposited the money in a drawer. "And what else can I help you with?" he said with a smile.

"We are quite satisfied for now, thank you," replied the preacher as he and the boys took their purchases outside and sat down on the edge of the porch.

The afternoon sun had melted behind the peak of the store roof, causing the front of the porch to rest in the shade. A barely-discernible breeze tiptoed across the porch just enough to stir the paper wrapper around the hoop cheese as it rested between Billy and Jubal. The preacher peeled back the top of the sardine can, took out a sardine, placed it between two saltines and passed it down to Billy who passed it down to Jubal. He then did the same with the Vienna sausage can, repeating the process with the saltines. He opened each bottle of Coca-Cola by using the opener nailed to the porch post next to the steps. Billy divided the slice of cheese into three parts. After everyone was served, they ate in silence, the only sound the soft rumble of Mr. Devlin's rocking chair as he watched them eat.

After watching his customers for a while, Mr. Devlin could no longer contain his curiosity. "What y'all doin' here?" he asked without preamble.

"Following the star," replied the preacher as he took a big drink of his Coca-Cola.

"What star? It's broad daylight, man."

"The spiritual star. Just as the wise men of old followed the star to the site of Jesus' birth, so we follow the star wherever it leads us to the site of the re-birth of lost souls."

"Uh huh. And that star led you to my store?"

"That is certainly a possibility."

"You think somebody's going to be reborn right here at Devlin's Store?"

"That possibility certainly exists."

"You a preacher?" Mr. Devlin probably asked that question because he couldn't see the sign painted on the truck since the only side that was painted was on the side away from the store.

"Some would call me that. I am a purveyor of the gospel."

"How do you propose to purvey at my store?"

"I believe the star has led us to that field yonder, to that spot of earth obviously set aside as the site of reincarnation for the human spirit, the place where the Lord will send those who seek relief from the oppression of their dreary existence and the burden of sin." The preacher rose from the porch and walked out to stand in front of the porch. As he looked out to the field past where the truck was parked, his voice rose as if he were standing in a church pulpit instead of beside a gas pump. "There lies the promised land!" he exclaimed, oblivious to the mixing of Old and New Testament metaphors.

He began to walk resolutely toward the open field, his head high as if looking to the heavens. When he reached the middle of the field, he turned back toward the store and the three people assembled there, raised both hands to the sky and proclaimed, "Here I make my stand! On this rock I will build my church!"

Mr. Devlin turned to the boys still seated on the porch steps. "What rock's he talking about? I've plowed that field for near 'bout forty years. There ain't no rocks out there. Is he crazy?"

Rock or no rocks, Mr. Branson had decided on the site of his tent service. He strode back to the store and instructed the boys to drive out into the field and set up the tent. The boys responded immediately and were soon unloading the tent canvas and placing poles and ropes that would change the field from a "fallow spot of earth to a flowering source of inspiration and redemption."

Mr. Devlin saw no need to give the preacher permission to set up in his field just as Mr. Branson had seen no need to ask for permission. The preacher joined the boys in getting everything set up. After the tent was raised, they placed a small platform at the end closest to the store, placed folding chairs in neat rows and strained to put a piano on the stage. They then took a long string of electric light bulbs and hung them around the edge of the tent, then placed a bigger light right over the middle of the stage.

Billy seemed to know exactly how to set up everything. Jubal followed instructions. After everything was set up, it occurred to Jubal that the real impetus for choosing that particular location for the tent was not so much Devine Inspiration as it was the availability of a power source to run the lights. The preacher took one end of a long electrical cord, pulled it through the front door of the store and plugged it into a socket next to the cash register.

It had taken most of the afternoon to get everything in place. As the sun began to go down, the heat abated somewhat and Mr. Devlin proceeded to close up his store. As he was leaving, Mr. Branson approached him. He had long ago shed his coat and tie; his shirt was soaked with sweat; his hair was wet and plastered to his head and he wiped his face with a handkerchief so wet it was ineffectual. However, he still possessed the confident swagger that he had exhibited when they had arrived at the store earlier that afternoon. He spoke to the storekeeper as he walked toward the old Chevrolet parked under a pine tree beside the store. "This has been a glorious day, Mr. Devlin, and we thank you for your willingness to join us in this effort to bring solace to the lost souls of this community."

"Now don't tie me into none of this," said the storekeeper.

"Y'all come in here and just took over, and I ain't had nothin' to do with none of it. I want everybody to know that. I ain't gonna charge you rent on the field and nothing for the electricity. Fact is, I was afraid if I tried to run you off, lightning might strike me seeing as it's the Lord's work you say you doing. I'm Presbyterian myself, and I don't put much stock in such shenanigans as this. Officially, I ain't for it or against it. Just so you'll know and anybody else that asks."

"Nonetheless, we are obliged. And there is one request. Could you direct me to the nearest town?"

"Brimley Springs is about five miles down that road there. It ain't much of a town, but it's got about anything a body could need. Don't tell anybody I sent you there." With that, Mr. Devlin got in his car and left.

The preacher turned to the boys and said, "Load up, boys, we will find us a bite to eat, a place to clean up and find out how to let folks know that we are here."

The town of Brimley Springs was a busy enough place during the day; but at night the life of the town shrunk to the one lighted building, Tom and Myrtle's Sinclair Station and Café. Tom and

Myrtle Ennis had been high-school sweethearts, married right after graduation. Tom joined the Army during the war while Myrtle operated the café. When he got back, he added the service station/garage. He was a good mechanic, she was a good cook and they prospered.

The preacher and the two boys were a pitiful-looking lot when they walked into the café. The heat and dust of the day had combined with the strenuous work of setting up the tent to create an image that tugged at the heartstrings of anyone as compassionate as Myrtle Ennis. Even the preacher's usually ebullient nature seemed subdued, but he still managed to find his oratorical eloquence as they walked into the café. "Good evening, madam," he said. "We are in search of some relief from our labors of the day. We would like to wash away the dust and weariness that has beset us and hope that you might provide some nourishment for our bodies."

"Well, if that means you want to wash up and get something to eat, the bathroom's over there; and when you get out, I'll take your order," said Myrtle as she wiped her hands with her apron and smiled at the grubby trio. They dutifully trailed into the bathroom.

When the three emerged from the bathroom, Myrtle was clearing the table where an older couple had just finished their meal.

"Just sit anywhere and I'll be right with you," she said, her arms full of dirty plates and saucers.

They sat silently until Myrtle returned and said, "We got a menu and you can look at if you want to; but I ain't cooked but one thing today, and that'd be meatloaf, mashed potatoes with gravy and some string beans. That comes with water or sweet tea and rolls."

"That will certainly suffice," said the preacher.

"You get to choose 'tween the sweet tea and water."

"Sweet tea will be fine."

Myrtle left and was back shortly with the three meals.

"If that tea ain't sweet enough for you, I got some little packets of sugar I can bring you. Used to just leave 'em on the table 'til it got to where people was just pickin' 'em up by the handful and totin' 'em outta here. Done the same thing with the bottles. Some people just ain't got no shame. What y'all doin' here?" she asked without preamble.

"I am a purveyor of the gospel," stated the preacher. "And these boys are my anointed minions. We have set up our tent at Mr. Devlin's store in anticipation of delivering God's word to the sinners of this community."

"Uh huh. You one of them travelin' preachers that goes around healing people kinda like Oral Roberts?"

"Brother Roberts is a colleague, but he has considerably larger resources than we."

"I listen to Oral Roberts on the radio all the time. Man's got a powerful voice. I went to see him one time over to Danville. Had a boil come up right up under this arm here, see?" she said as she lifted her right arm and pointed down the short sleeve of her dress. "Didn't get to actually have him work on it. Too many people in that line, and I ain't got no patience in the first place. Come home and my Granny Jacobs cut on it. Hurt like hell, but she got all the stuff out and it healed right up."

Despite their initial hunger, the meal seemed to lose its appeal for the diners. In a real effort to change the subject, Mr. Branson said, "We are in need of some assistance in our mission. Do you know where we might find someone interested in playing the piano for our service?"

"Miss Sally Cooper right down at the Baptist church can play. She teaches music at the school too. But I can tell you right now, Miss Sally ain't gonna take up with no tent revival. She is way too dignified for that. What you need is a good band. Somebody that can get your congregation movin' and clappin'. I expect you'd like to get 'em feelin' good enough to open their pocketbooks, wouldn't you?"

"Well, that proposal certainly has some merit," ventured the preacher. "I suspect you have somebody in mind."

"You suspect right. As a matter of fact, my brother Clement has been stayin' at my house for 'bout two weeks now waitin' for just such an opportunity to come along. Him and three more fellows have been travelin' around the country playin' bluegrass for all kinds of occasions. Told me they played some with Bill Monroe and

Mac Wiseman. I don't believe it 'cause they ain't that good. I don't know that they ever played for a tent revival, but I bet they can. You know, the Lord moves in mysterious ways, preacher. And just between me and you and the Lord, I'm ready for 'em to move on. You know what I mean?"

"Yes, madam, I believe I do. Why don't you have them report to our site some time tomorrow morning for a brief audition? We can probably work out something mutually beneficial. I would ask one other favor of you. We have a poster in the truck which we would like to place in your window here to make folks aware of the spiritual opportunity we are making available. Would you let us leave one here?" the preacher asked.

"By all means," answered Myrtle. "In fact, if you think you might could take on this bunch, I'll spread some more posters 'round town."

"Thank you. I appreciate your assistance. Now, how much do I owe you for this fine meal?" he asked.

"Nothing, not a thing. It's worth the price of a meal or three to get Clement and his friends outta my house. 'Sides y'all didn't hardly eat enough to pay for. I can just hold it over 'til tomorrow."

As the group started to leave the restaurant, Jubal saw a pay phone on the wall behind the cash register. He realized that he had not called his mother since leaving Taggart; and, although he had left her a note, he knew that she'd be worried about him. He said,

"Mr. Branson, while y'all get the posters out, I think I need to call my mother." It had only been two days, but it seemed he had been gone for two weeks. He didn't even know how far he had gone, only that he was headed south toward Ft. Bragg and his brother.

He picked up the heavy, black phone handle, unwound the cord attached to the coin box and dialed zero. After two buzzes, the operator came on the line, "May I help you?"

"Yes, ma'am," he replied. "I need to place a collect call to Mrs. Jane Simpson in Taggart, Virginia. The number is TA3-3954."

"And whom shall I say is calling?"

"This is her son, Jubal. She'll know who it is."

After about two rings, Jubal heard his mother answer the phone, "Hello."

The operator said, "I have a collect call from Jubal for…"

"Jubal, Jubal. Where are you? I've been so worried!"

"I take it you will accept the call?" asked the operator.

"Yes, oh, yes!" exclaimed Jane, her voice brimming with excitement almost to the point of tears.

"I'm alright, Mama. I'm still on my way to get up with Mac. A preacher and his son gave me a ride, and I'm doing fine. We just ate supper, and we'll have a preaching service tomorrow; then we'll be moving on to Fort Bragg just like I told you in my note."

"Oh, Jubal. I was so worried. You can't be joining the army. You're not old enough, and Mac doesn't even know what you're doing. I called the sheriff and he's had deputies out looking for you, and Leon and Raymond have been out driving all over the place with that light flashing on top of the hearse. I've been frantic!" Then her voice took on as stern a tone as she could muster. "You need to come on back here right now, young man, before something terrible happens." Then her voice broke, "I want you home, Jubal. Your daddy is gone; Mac has gone. You're my baby. I want you home."

For the first time, Jubal's resolution to join his brother began to weaken. He had seldom heard his mother cry. He was torn between joining his brother whom he saw as fighting alone against an undefined enemy in a foreign country or returning home to care for the mother who had always cared for him. What kind of son would he be to leave his mother crying for his return? What kind of brother would he be to leave his only brother to fight and face death alone in a foreign country? He struggled in silence as the sound of his mother's anguished sobs seeped and whispered through the phone. Finally, he said, "It'll be alright, Mama. I'll come back and bring Mac with me. You'll see. I'll call you tomorrow from Mr. Devlin's store." And he hung up the phone before he could change his mind.

Chapter 6

The Shenandoah Ramblers arrived at the revival tent shortly after noon the next day. They arrived unencumbered by money, sobriety or theology. Their only motivation for being there was the unfounded promise of the possibility of maybe getting some money by playing at the tent service. With that tenuous intimation, they approached the revival tent of the Reverend Josiah Branson as he rested on the portable cot he had slept on the night before.

The car they arrived in was an old Dodge, apparently a slate-blue color under the heavy coat of dust. Its most distinctive characteristic was the bass fiddle strapped to the top.

They were a motley crew. It was apparent that Myrtle's hospitality did not extend to washing and ironing. Each wore a long-sleeve white—actually, almost tan—dress shirt, sleeves rolled up to the elbow and dark woolen dress pants that at some time had been part of a suit, along with black-and-white spectator shoes. Their hair was plastered to their heads with enough hair oil to grease a freight train, and it had been at least three or four days since any one of them had shaved. All together they fell into the general category of deep dishevelment.

The preacher sat up from his cot and looked at the four men as they approached. He assumed they were the band Myrtle had told him about since there was a bass fiddle tied to the top of the car. He had not known exactly what to expect; but the scene before him was more like an apparition stirring the dust of the dry field, the wind sweeping away the evidence of their tracks even as they walked desultorily into the shade of the tent.

"You the preacher?" asked the man leading the group.

"I'm Reverend Josiah Branson," answered the preacher. "And who might you be?" he asked although he knew who they were.

"I'm Clement Todd, and these others here's the rest of the Shenandoah Ramblers. I'm the brother Myrtle told you about. She said you might have a job for us?"

"Yes, I might. I told Myrtle that I would need a small audition. Did you bring your instruments?"

"Oh, yes, sir. Got 'em in the car. You want us to get 'em out?"

"I believe that would be the next necessary step toward hearing you play," replied Josiah with just a touch of polite sarcasm.

All four men turned and walked toward the car with the same lackadaisical gait with which they had approached the tent. They returned at the same speed.

As they unpacked their instruments, Clement asked, "Whatcha wanta hear?"

"Whatever you choose that will be representative of your repertoire will be fine," said the preacher.

"What if we just play something we know?"

"That will be fine," said the preacher as he sat down on the cot.

"By the way," said Clement, "this here is Milford on banjo, Curtis on mandolin, Craven plays the fiddle and I play this guitar and sometimes one of us might play the bass fiddle. It's back at the car. Had another feller played it regular, but he got to drinkin' so bad I had to let him go. The Trailways bus driver wouldn't let him take the bass on the bus so we swapped him a pint of liquor for it. Kinda crowds the car though, so we tied it on top."

After a short tuning period, the four stood side by side and at a nod from Clement began to play.

I wandered so aimless, life filled with sin
I couldn't let my dear savior in
Then Jesus came like a stranger in the night Praise the Lord I
saw the light.

I saw the light, I saw the light
No more darkness, no more night
Now I'm so happy no sorrow in sight Praise the Lord I saw the
light.

Their fingers flew up and down the frets of their instruments like long-legged spiders on a hot fire poker. Each instrument was in exact rhythm with the others, and the vocal harmony was so tight it was almost like one voice.

The preacher sat transfixed, taken aback by the transformation. Somehow the scraggly band had mingled into a single sound so beautiful that their scruffy attire and unkempt appearance faded away.

I was a fool to wander and stray
Straight is the gate and narrow the way Now I have traded the
wrong for the right Praise the Lord I saw the light.

As soon as they finished the song, the vision disappeared from the preacher's eyes; and he saw again the rough quartet sweating from their exertion in the summer heat.

"That ain't exactly a church song, you know," said Clement. "It's a old Hank Williams song. We played some with him one time down in Alabama. We can't sing it as good as he done it but... well, there ain't nobody can sing it like Hank." Clement spoke with such humility and earnestness that Josiah Branson admitted, "You are angels unaware of yourselves. You're hired. Go ahead and get cleaned up as best you can and be back here tonight at 7:00 for the service. Plan to sing several songs." Then he added, almost as an afterthought, "Consumption of alcohol in any form, even as inspiration, is not an option." He then turned abruptly and walked away from the group. They, in turn, walked back to their car without saying a word. Somehow, accidentally or on purpose, nobody had said anything about paying the band.

Jubal and Billy had watched the audition of the Shenandoah Ramblers from the back of the tent. Both sat in wooden folding chairs, their arms spread across the back of the chairs in front of them.

"Don't think we ever had anybody like them in a service before. Might bring in some more people, or it might run some off. Never can tell 'bout people, you know. Some folks think that kinda music is the work of the devil," observed Billy. "Then again, some folks might come just to hear the music since they're not particularly interested in listening to a sermon. And some might come 'cause they got nothing better to do. Not a lot to choose from around here, I 'spect."

"I like 'em," said Jubal. "What are we going to do with the piano though?"

"Leave it right where it is 'til Pa tells us to move it. No need to take on work unless we have to," was Billy's philosophical reply.

As if in response to Billy's thoughts, the preacher called to the boys, "You boys move this piano to the back of the stage, and let's set up this microphone and speakers. And, Billy, don't forget to put some tape on that amplifier cord."

For the next hour or so, the three worked at completing the setup for the night's service. When they had finished, Mr. Branson said, "Now it's time for a break. Let us repair to Mr. Devlin's establishment and avail ourselves of refreshment."

Since they had not eaten since their meager breakfast, the "refreshments" served as the meal for the day. It consisted of pretty much the same thing they had eaten the day before, but their hunger paid no attention to the repeated menu.

While the preacher stayed inside and talked with Mr. Devlin, Billy and Jubal returned to the shade of the tent to eat their meal. The heat seemed to be bearing down with not even a hint of a breeze to provide any relief. They pulled up chairs to the edge of the stage and used the stage as a temporary dinner table.

"There'll be some girls at the service tonight, you know," said Billy.

"How you know?" asked Jubal.

"Always is," was the matter-of-fact reply.

"You ever talk to any?"

"Oh, yeah, lots of 'em."

"What do you talk about?"

"We talk about the weather; then I tell what hymns we're going to sing. They usually real interested in that, you know. Then they'll ask me where I'm from and I tell 'em no place in particular, that I'm just a world traveler who goes wherever the wind blows. Gives 'em a sorta romantic view. Sounds better than 'where the Lord leads me' like Pa says. Then if they want to get real specific, I tell 'em I been as far as Atlanta, Georgia and Memphis, Tennessee. By then I got 'em in the palm of my hand."

"What happens after you got 'em in the palm of your hand?" Jubal asked with some anticipation.

"Nothing yet. Just about the time I get to that point, Pa starts the service and it's hard to get up with 'em after that, you know."

"Bet that's how your dad met your mom, huh? At a service?"

"Don't know. Pa never talks about her. Just says for me to know she was a good woman. I don't know anything about her and any time I ask him Pa just repeats that she was a good woman. Miss Eberline, one of my teachers back in grade school, said I needed to give them some medical information in case of an emergency; and they'd have to get my mother's records too. Pa told her there weren't any. I guess I'll have to find out from somebody else. You really lucky to have your mama. What happen to your daddy?"

Jubal didn't answer right away. He suddenly felt homesick for his mother, his brother, for Taggart, even for Leon McKoy. "I was real little when my daddy died. He got killed during the war. I don't remember much about him, but we had lots of pictures and Mama's told me all about him. She said me and my brother Mac look a lot like Daddy. I can't tell that from the pictures, but I like to think so anyway." Again, he lapsed into silence, then said matter-of-factly, "I gotta call Mama."

Jubal started walking over to the store. He knew Mr. Devlin would let him use the telephone to call his mother. He just wanted to tell her he was alright, to reassure her so she wouldn't worry. He knew if he could get to Mac, his brother could convince his mother that it was the proper thing to do for both of them to join up and fight for their country even if they didn't know who the enemy was.

As he walked across the hot hay field to the store, he recalled what the preacher back at the church in Taggart had said at the Fourth of July celebration, "God, family and country are all worth fighting for." Jubal wondered if that were the order of importance. He had only a cursory knowledge about God and even less about the United States of America, but he sure knew about family. As far as Jubal was concerned, if you cared about your family, the other two automatically fell in place. You fight for one, you fight for the other two.

Just as Jubal stepped up on the porch of the store, a car drove up and parked behind Mr. Devlin's car next to the side of the store. It was an old car, black, with all the windows rolled down. The dust that was following the car billowed through those windows as the vehicle came to a stop. The driver who got out of the car almost before the dust settled was a short lady of about fifty years of age wearing a black-and-white polka-dot dress, a small black straw hat and *sensible*, low-heeled shoes. She carried a purple pocketbook about the size of a suitcase, apparently filled to the optimum since she practically dragged it across the dirt toward the store porch.

Mr. Devlin greeted her before she got to the porch. "Why, Miss Cooper, what brings you out here? 'Course, I'm always glad to see you."

"J.C., I hear that a bunch of the devil's disciples are going to play God's music for this…this…vagabond church service tonight, and I have come to see that some modicum of real spirituality accompanies even this modest effort to spread God's word."

"Well, Miss Cooper, I don't know about all that. All I know is that a pretty good bluegrass band showed up this morning, played a little music for the preacher and left. You'll have to ask Preacher Branson about anything else."

"Plan to do just that. Where can I find him?"

"Right over there under the tent," said Devlin as he pointed to the prominent tent, visible to all but a blind eye set up in the pasture.

"Jubal, why don't you take Miss Cooper over and introduce her to the preacher?"

Jubal nodded his acceptance of Mr. Devlin's request and began to walk back toward the tent. "Young man… Jubal, is it? The courteous thing to do would be to take my arm and assist me across this rubble-strewn field. I dare not fall. It could be fatal to a woman of my delicate condition."

Jubal stepped to the side of Miss Cooper who placed her left arm in the crook of Jubal's right and proceeded toward the tent with

67

as much dignity as could be arranged under the circumstances.

The preacher saw the couple approaching as he sat in a wooden folding chair, his feet propped up on the edge of the stage. He stood up and immediately walked out to greet them.

As they came together on the edge of the tent, Jubal said, "Miss Cooper, this is Reverend Branson." Mr. Branson extended his hand, and Jubal placed Miss Cooper's hand in the preacher's. Jubal had only seen one other escort, and that had been at a wedding where the father of the bride escorted his daughter down the aisle; and when the preacher had said, "Who gives this woman?" he had placed her hand in the groom's. Not a bad example but probably not even close to being appropriate for this occasion.

"How do you do, madam?" greeted the preacher.

"I am doing well, thank you," was the reply. "However, before we dismiss young Jacob, I must give him a little bit of instruction as to gentlemanly etiquette." Then she turned to Jubal. "Young man, I appreciate your assisting me across the field. However, as a matter of reference, in the future when introducing two people always present the gentleman to the lady, saying her name first, then invert the process. And, just so you'll know, the gentleman does not shake hands with a lady unless she offers her hand for that purpose. A simple bow from the gentleman is appropriate. I hope that will be helpful to you as you become more socially adept."

"Thank you, ma'am. I'll keep that in mind," said Jubal, thinking that such a situation was probably not going to be a frequent occurrence.

"As for you, Mr. Branson, I have come to offer my assistance in providing music for congregational singing tonight. I understand that you have contacted a string band to play. Frankly, I think that is an abomination to allow such music to be played in a house of worship, no matter how shoddy and temporary the church may be. Even if the occasion is ephemeral, for that short time it is God's house and should receive the same reverence as the greatest cathedral."

"I take it that you play the piano," said Branson, trying to be as cordial as possible. "I would be pleased to hear a selection which you think would be appropriate for congregational singing."

"Sir, I have a degree in music from the Flora McDonald Seminary in Red Springs, North Carolina. I have been the official accompanist and choir director at the Brimley Springs Baptist Church for nearly forty years and I have taught private lessons to hundreds of young people for as long a period. My credentials speak for me, so I have no intention of being auditioned by a fly-by-night cleric whose own qualifications may not be acceptable to those who seek clarification or explanation of God's word. Do I make myself clear, Mr. Branson?"

"Yes, ma'am, you certainly do. What I meant to ask was, do you have some particular hymns in mind for the congregation to sing?"

"Of course, I do. As a matter of fact, I took the liberty of putting together an order of service which I would suggest you use." As she handed a handwritten order of service to the preacher, she added, "I will, of course, put together my own prelude which should not concern you. I suggest we open with 'Victory In Jesus' as the call to worship, 'All Hail The Power Of Jesus' Name' as the second hymn, 'I Surrender All' for the offertory and 'Just As I Am' for the invitation. That has six verses, you know, which gives people time to make up their minds; and, of course, we can always slow it down if we need to. I will do this at no charge since it is my Christian duty."

Reverend Branson and Miss Cooper were still standing where Jubal had left them at the edge of the tent. When Miss Cooper finished her introductory remarks, Reverend Branson said, "Let's sit down over here, Miss Cooper," as he indicated the front row of chairs. "I really do appreciate your willingness to help with the service, but I have already contracted with the band to play tonight. Do you think you could share the musical aspects of the service with them?"

"Certainly not. Although I hear they are accomplished musicians in their own field, I come to bury Caesar, not to praise him. Those barroom balladeers have no place here, and you will not need them now that I am here." With that she stood and started walking back toward her car, then turned to Jubal who had been sitting on the edge of the platform and said, "Come, Jubal, help me back to my car, please."

Josiah Branson was not accustomed to being overwhelmed, but Miss Sally Cooper had conquered him. As he watched Jubal and Miss Cooper walk across the field, he realized that he had not been able to even put up a defense. Now he was left to find a way to tell the Shenandoah Ramblers that they would not be playing that night. He had no telephone number and no other way to reach them. He would just have to confront them after they arrived for the service.

Chapter 7

As evening approached the revival site, a soft breeze began to blow across the field. Little puffs of dust blew into the tent from one side, exhausting themselves before exiting on the other side. There was a calming silence that seemed to relax the preacher and his boys as they prepared for the service. Mr. Devlin, in a change of heart, had decided to lend his support to the trio and had his wife fix some sandwiches to which he added three Coca Colas. They were eating their evening meal as the first worshipers arrived.

The visitors arrived in the same kind of clothes they wore to church on Sunday: some in coats and ties, some in long-sleeved white shirts and freshly-washed bib overalls. Some of the ladies wore white dresses with a shawl to ward off the possible nighttime chill. They chatted with each other after settling in the back rows.

Miss Cooper returned, looking pretty much like she had left except for a different hat, a light-green straw that made her look like one of the pictures of a leprechaun Jubal had seen in the World Book Encyclopedia.

She immediately sat down at the piano, sorted through her purple bag for some sheet music and began to play. The songs were familiar to Jubal. They were the same songs he had learned back at the church in Taggart. He sang them every Sunday as he stood beside his mother. When Miss Cooper played "Jesus Loves the Little Children," he softly sang along. He had learned that one in Bible School and had sung it with his class at bible school commencement. The memory made him realize that he had not made the phone call to his mother because of the interruption of Miss Cooper's arrival. He vowed to call her as soon as the service was over.

The tent was beginning to fill up with people. Myrtle had evidently done a good job of getting the word out. That was a concern for the preacher. Myrtle had kept her end of the bargain, but he was going to have to tell her brother's band they weren't going to play after all. He would have to think up a compromise.

He didn't have long to think before the band arrived. Even as darkness reduced the visibility, it was easy to distinguish their car since it still had the bass fiddle tied on top.

They pulled up right behind the platform and got out immediately. Billy and Jubal had left the tent side down at the back side of the platform. Mr. Branson had said it helped with the acoustics and gave a background so people could see him better. As the band members emerged, it was apparent that they had gone to considerable effort to improve their appearance. They all wore grey suits with white piping around the edge of the coats and a stripe down the pant legs. They wore shined and polished black cowboy boots and grey, wide-brimmed western hats. They didn't look at all like the bedraggled group of that afternoon.

Clement looked around, searching for the preacher, finally seeing him standing at the side of the tent greeting visitors. As he walked over toward the preacher, Clement could tell that all the congregants were watching him; but Miss Cooper was pretending not to notice and continued playing the piano.

The preacher turned and saw Clement walking toward him. He was pleasantly surprised to see the change in the musician's appearance. He was even more determined to work out some kind of arrangement that would justify their effort to literally clean up their act.

"Clement, my boy, you look wonderfully well. My, my, what a change from this afternoon. I commend you on your transformation. However, I must tell you that there has been a slight change in the order of service. As you see, Miss Cooper has generously offered to provide the musical accompaniment for the service, and she absolutely refuses to share the stage with you. So I have decided that we should provide you with your own personal venue for your marvelous performance that will allow you to display your music without distraction. I plan to announce that, following the service tonight, The Shenandoah Ramblers will perform. This will be a wonderful opportunity for you, and I will still pay you what we promised earlier."

"We still get paid?" was the immediate response from Clement.

"Oh, certainly. The same as we talked about before: ten per cent of the offering."

"Twenty-five per cent,"

"Twenty"

Clements's initial response was the result of his previous experience with promoters. Over the years he had heard every possible excuse for canceling a performance and had way too many promoters leave town before paying the band. It was enough to make a man turn to drink. He knew that the preacher was not a promoter; but when it came to money, Clement saw no distinction.

"You boys just make yourselves comfortable; and as soon as the service is over, the stage is yours," said the preacher.

As Clement walked back to tell the other band members of the change in plans, the preacher mounted the platform, welcomed the congregation and asked them to sing "Bringing in the Sheaves"— as chosen by Miss Cooper—on page 31 of the old hymn books placed in their chairs. After the song was sung and the people were again seated, he said, "Folks, we have a real treat for you tonight. You know, God works his wonders in mysterious ways sometimes and tonight is such an occasion. After the service tonight, you are invited to attend a free performance by the Shenandoah Ramblers. God has made this possible. Just this afternoon, these men were poor wastrels cast away with all hope lost. Tonight they are here transformed, evidence that hope exists anywhere and everywhere, anytime and all the time. See them for yourself after the service."

The congregation applauded. Miss Cooper sat stone-faced and still.

The service proceeded along the usual lines, following the order of service that Miss Cooper had given the preacher. At the appropriate time, Billy and Jubal passed straw baskets among the congregation, then delivered the baskets and the money to the preacher. Mr. Branson's sermon was long on exhortation to prayer with the firm assurance that hell awaited all those who failed to succumb to the will of God immediately. Murmurs of "amen" sifted through the congregation; hands were raised in supplication, acknowledging a sinful past and entreating forgiveness.

As the preacher got more and more excited, the hot afternoon breeze that had previously cooled the humid air began to blow with increasing intensity until the two elements—man and nature—seemed to stir the congregation. People began to stand, waving their arms more vigorously, the "amens" louder and more frequent.

When the preacher finally asked all who sought forgiveness of their sins to come forward and kneel with him, just about everybody in the place started walking toward the little raised platform.

In all the emotional chaos, nobody noticed the frayed electric cord that ran from Mr. Devlin's store to the small amplifier that pushed the sound of Mr. Branson's voice to the speakers mounted on the side of the stage. A lady with a cane was moving as quickly as she could toward the platform when her cane caught the cord just enough to move it. A small spark leapt from the frayed cord, then landed on the dried grass. Almost immediately, a small flame began.

In just a few seconds, the wind whipped the small flame into a blaze that caught the tent flap, then sped toward the chairs and the dried grass underneath them. As the fire roared up the side of the tent, screams erupted from the crowd. Someone shouted, "It's the rapture and I ain't been baptized! Lord, take my word for it! I'm a believer!"

People rushed out of the tent, some pushing those in front of them to the ground as they clamored to escape the encroaching flames. The fire ate up the tinder-dry grass and engulfed the ragged tent with a roar. The flames lit up the night sky as a storm of people sped away in their cars while some ran away, leaving their cars behind.

Billy and Jubal had been at the back of the tent. When the fire started, Billy ran out the side, then toward the other end of the tent calling for his father.

Jubal's first thought was, "I didn't call Mama." He started running toward Devlin's store which happened to be away from the path of the fire. When he got to the door, he found it locked. In desperation he looked for some way to get in. He needed to call his mother; he knew she could fix any situation.

He looked around for something he could use to break a

window. At the edge of the porch, he saw a cement block. Just as he reached to pick it up and hurl it through the window, a strong arm grasped him, knocking the block from his hand.

Clement Todd said, "Come on, boy, git in this car 'fore your ass gits burnt to a crisp."

Jubal was so surprised by the abrupt rescue that he offered no resistance as his liberator pushed him into the back seat of the car with the bass fiddle still strapped to the top of it.

Dust from the speeding car mixed with the smoke from the fire created a maelstrom so thick it was almost impossible for Milford, the banjo player/driver, to see where he needed to go to get away from it all. Suddenly a strong puff of wind shifted the direction of the cloud of dust and smoke. In the brief absence of any obstruction to his vision, Milford saw a big spotted goat standing directly in front of the car. He slammed on the brakes just in time to keep from hitting the goat and a tall, sturdy pine tree immediately behind him.

"What da hell…?" exclaimed Clement.

Jubal recognized the goat. It was the one he had left back at the preacher's house.

"What's a goat doin' out here?" asked a stupefied Curtis. *Saving our lives*, thought Jubal.

"It don't matter. There's the road over there," directed Clement. "Git on it and let's git outta here."

As the car spun around, dust again covered the goat.

Chapter 8

It's frustrating to be hurtling down a curvy mountain road at a high rate of speed at night, particularly when you don't know where you are or where you are going. For Jubal the anxiety was amplified by the confusion of three people yelling conflicting instructions at a driver barely able to see the road.

At some point Milford decided that he had had enough. He abruptly stopped the car in what was probably the middle of the road and said, "By God, I'm doin' the best I can. I can't hardly see past the hood ornament. So if any one of you smart asses can do better, git up here right now and do it!" With that exclamation, he opened the car door, got out and stood by the side of the road with his hands on his hips.

A stunned silence was the only response. After a moment, Clement said calmly, "Come on, Milford, git back in the car. We was just over-wrought, you know. We just wanted to git away 'fore that fire got to so we couldn't git away. It's startin' to clear up some now. Come on, you the driver of this outfit, duly-appointed and rectified."

Mollified by the recognition of his assigned position, Milford got back in the car, which he began to ease slowly down the mountain road as the smoke became less and less dense.

After about ten minutes of riding in silence, Craven asked, "I don't want to challenge the mental ability of this bunch, but you reckon anybody can tell me where the hell we are?"

"I don't know exactly," replied Milford, "but I do know we are near 'bout out of gas. I been savin' gas by coastin' a lot down these hills; but we startin' to level out now so I know we can't go much further 'til we put some juice in this thing."

"We bound to be close to the North Carolina line 'cause Myrtle said she gits the gas for the service station from King, which is just on the other side of the line; and since I believe we been goin' south down these hills, we ought to be somewheres around there. There ain't that many roads in and outa these hills," declared Clement with just a smattering of logic as he pulled a small bottle of clear liquid out of his coat pocket and took a big swallow.

"Let me have a swig of that stuff, Clement," said Craven. "My nerves is near 'bout shot what with a fire burnin' up a church meetin', a goat 'pearin' like a ghost and Milford drivin' like a blind man; I need somethin' to settle my body down."

Jubal was sitting silently in the back seat, wedged between Clement and Craven. No one in the car had even acknowledged his presence so when he spoke up, it might have startled them a little.

"That stuff'll kill you, you know," he said.

"What do you know about it, boy? You an authority on

moonshine?" Craven asked with a little laugh.

"Nope, I ain't sure about it, but Mama said liquor was the downfall of many a good man. And my science teacher told us that moonshine would burn if you set a match to it. Stands to reason that if it'll burn from a match, it's probably not good for your stomach."

"Pass it up here, Craven," said Curtis. "I'll take my chances."

The full darkness of the night soon engulfed the crowded old car as it wound its way down the hills. Eventually the glow of a full moon shown through the cloudless sky, the ridges of the hills silhouetted like a rumpled bedcover before them. It may have been that image plus the moonshine that caused them all to get quiet, some snoring. Only Milford, fighting against slumber, kept looking down the road searching for a gas station.

The wind blowing through the windows created a hum that joined with the sound of the engine, adding to the inducement to sleep. Inevitably the hum was broken by a sudden chug of the motor, a cough that proved Milford's prediction true; they were out of gas. As the four passengers woke from their slumber, Milford said quietly, "I told you we needed gas."

Surprisingly, there was no rancorous response. Whether from weariness or from the knowledge that any other response was useless, they all got out of the car as if their exit would further identify or clarify their situation.

"There ain't no tellin' how far it is to a gas station," said

Clement. "We got two choices: one, one of us can start walkin'; or two, we can just stay here to mornin' and somebody comes along. Whatcha wanta do?"

Milford was the first to speak, "Well, I can tell ya I ain't walkin' nowhere. I been drivin' while y'all be sleepin', and my weary ass is goin' to sleep one way or t'other. Now that's just the way it is." And with that announcement, he crawled into the back seat and was almost immediately asleep.

"I am against walkin'," said Craven. "Walkin' along a road at night is just a invitation for somebody to come along and knock you in the head and take everything you got. I say we stay here 'til somebody comes along."

"I tell you what, boys. Sittin' here 'side the road with a bass fiddle tied to the top of that car is just a invitation for some no-good to come along, kill us and take the fiddle and run. I think we ought to at least take the fiddle down, no matter what else we do," was Curtis' suggestion.

"Now who the hell would steal a bass fiddle, Curtis? That's the dumbest thing I ever heard of," was Clement's authoritative response.

"You got anymore moonshine?" asked Jubal.

"Moonshine? What's the matter, boy? You need a little drink to keep the boogers away?" laughed Clement.

"Nope, I ain't afraid," he answered. "But if you got some, you might could pour it in the gas tank and get us a little farther down the road, maybe to a station. I've heard that works sometimes."

The validity of moonshine as a substitute for gasoline is questionable, to say the least. Cartoons are probably the only actual known source of such information and Jubal's sole reference. But under the circumstances, that was enough for the weary group.

Clement dutifully extracted two quart jars of the alcohol from the trunk of the car and poured it slowly into the gas tank. There is no record of the recipe used to create that particular batch of moonshine; but whatever the combination of ingredients, it was sufficient to start the engine.

With some excitement, the whole crew got back in the car; and the over-extended auto proceeded down the road erratically, depending on how the engine was processing the exotic fuel.

"What ails this thing now?" asked an agitated Clement of no one in particular. "How come it's jumping like this?"

Encouraged by his unexpected knowledge of moonshine as automobile fuel, Jubal began to expound on his new area of expertise. "It's probably the sugar that was used in distilling the shine that's messing up the carburetor. The amount of combustible alcohol ain't steady enough to keep it running regular."

"And how is it you got to know so much about moonshine and cars, boy?" asked Clement.

Jubal knew he had to come up with some explanation to

maintain his credibility with his new friends. He actually knew almost nothing about cars. He had heard Mac talking about carburetors and gaskets and radiators, but he didn't have any idea how it was all connected to make a car run; and he had even less information about moonshine. The only thing he knew about the illegal whiskey was what he had read in the Taggert paper about the sheriff arresting moonshiners and busting up their stills. So he put it all together as best he could.

"My brother runs moonshine back home. Got the fastest car around. Makes good money too," he said with as much confidence as he could muster, given his ignorance.

"That a fact?" questioned Clement. "You ever ride with 'im?"

"Oh, yeah, lots a times. I seen him put that real good, high-class moonshine in his car. Man, that thing'd near 'bout run out from under you."

"Well, it don't appear to be working too good on this car."

"'Cause that's probably not high-class moonshine you put in there," continued Jubal confidently, building on his tenuous credibility.

"Hmm. That could be, boy. That could be," mused Clement as he sat back in the seat and gazed out at the early-morning sun beginning to peek over the hills.

With the dawn came the sighting of a small service station, the flying red horse trademark of the Mobil oil company swinging in the early morning breeze.

"Thank God A'mighty!" shouted Milford. "Some real gas!" He pulled up to the pump and stopped, the glass bulb on top of the pump indicating that there was, indeed, gasoline to be had.

The inhabitants of the old car emerged slowly, walking stiffly, lifting their arms in a freedom of movement denied them for too long. The station itself was a small cinder-block structure painted white. A big double window looked out on the roadside, and a small wooden door with the top half made of paned glass stood closed to the travelers. The left side of the building was apparently the garage portion of the service station. A wide, folding door was padlocked to the cement floor.

"Anybody here?" shouted Curtis. No answer. He began to walk down the right side of the building, calling out for someone to pump some gasoline.

"How's anybody 'spect to make a livin' out of a gas station if they ain't never open?" asked Craven, apparently not considering the early hour.

"I gotta pee," said Curtis as matter-of-factly as he could, given the real urgency of the situation. He started toward the back of the store, fumbling to unzip his pants while walking. The mention of nature's call seemed to stimulate the need in the other members of the group as they followed Curtis toward his makeshift latrine.

"Hey, what'a you think you're doin' there?" came a startling cry. All five turned in unison to see a big man clad in coveralls striding toward them from across the field beside the store. "That ain't no public latrine back there, you know."

"When you gotta go, you gotta go, mister," responded Clement. "Don't mean no harm."

"Well, I got a toilet in the station here. I was just gonna open up," said the man as he walked to the door of the station and unlocked it.

As each man waited in line, then went into the small restroom, the station owner asked, "Y'all want some gas, I reckon. Fill it up?"

"Yeah, might as well," answered Curtis, the spokesman by default since Clement was in the restroom.

As each man left the restroom, he picked up some snacks off a bread rack which stood against the wall, then pulled a cold soft drink from the bottom of a large chest with cold water swirling slowly around the bottom. Jubal was the last to use the restroom so he only heard the last part of the conversation as he went over to get a honey bun and a Pepsi.

"What do you mean, you ain't got no money? You told me to fill it up. How were you plannin' to pay for it?" asked the station manager as he shouted across the cash register.

"Well, I, uh… well, I … to tell you the truth, mister, I was in such a hurry to get into that toilet, I forgot we didn't have no money. I wasn't plannin' on tellin' you no lie; it just won't my priority at the time."

"Listen, I don't care about your bodily functions one way or the other. The fact still remains, I got to git something for that gas I put in your car, or else you gonna have to git out there and siphon every bit of it back into a gas can. Now what you gonna do about it?"

Clement was at a loss for words. The other members of the group started easing out of the store and casually got into the car. Only Jubal remained standing beside Clement.

"Clement, what about that high-class moonshine you got in the car? Reckon it ought to be worth a tank of gas?" asked Jubal.

Clement's brow furrowed as he looked down at Jubal. He was startled at first by the sound of the boy's voice. He was surprised that Jubal was still there. But the real silent question in his mind was, "What moonshine?" They had poured the only two quarts they had into the car.

The station manager also had a question. "You got moonshine with you?"

Jubal answered, "Yes, sir. The best you ever tasted. First class is what it is. It's worth well more than a tank of gas. 'Course, we ain't got but one jar left. It was give to us by some folks that we played for at the state capital. They wouldn't have nothin' 'less it was the best. They were all Republicans, you know."

"Uh huh. Republican moonshine. Never had any myself. Didn't even know there was any such thing," mused the station manager.

"Tell you what I'll do. I'll take that jar of moonshine for the gas and all the food y'all got too. Just this time, mind you. If you ever come back by here again, don't even think about stoppin'."

"I'll run and get it, Clement. Y'all just stay right here," said Jubal, indicating that he needed to go to the car alone.

As soon as he got to the car, he opened the back door and took out the empty quart jar that had once held the gasoline substitute.

"Get the motor runnin', Milford. We going to be leaving real soon," he said as he dashed over to the side of the station and filled the jar with water from the spigot that jutted out of the side of the wall, sniffed the liquid to make sure there was still enough smell of the strong brew, then screwed the lid on tight.

Jubal walked back into the station and placed the jar on the counter.

"You can just smell that good stuff before you even open it. Just take a whiff of the lid. That's the kind of stuff you save for special occasions to share with your friends," he said as he and Clement walked quickly toward the door. "Be a shame to open it right now and spoil it for later."

As soon as Jubal and Clement got in the car, they looked back through the station door and saw the man unscrew the lid off the quart jar. "Let's go, Milford. Right now," said Clement.

Small rocks and dust spun from the tires of the now-rejuvenated Dodge as Milford shifted the gears on the steering-wheel column with a grinding noise that reminded them all that neither their driver nor their automobile was ready to outrun the law.

"Oh, Lord, help us," moaned Clement. "Jubal done made us outlaws. That man's goin' to sic the law on us for sure. We'll be hunted down like Dillinger, shot to pieces by machine guns!"

"No he won't," said Jubal. "What's he goin' to tell the law? That a kid came by and traded a fake jar of moonshine for a tank of gas? I don't believe he'll let anybody know about that, least of all the law."

Jubal had begun to see how the creative use of the truth could be useful.

Chapter 9

Miss Jane had told us to call her at least every two or three hours. Each time we were to get further instruction and find out if she had heard anything from Jubal. We had not seen a pay phone since we left Taggart. As that fateful Sunday was coming to a close, we stopped at a service station about four hours into our journey. The pay phone stood apart from the station under a large oak tree. Leon left the door of the booth open as much to let in the cool afternoon breeze as to allow me to hear one side of the conversation.

"Jane, this is Leon. Have you heard anything from Jubal?.... Well, don't you worry. I'm sure he'll call as soon as he can....Yes, he knows how to use the phone. He's not such a little boy, you know.... No, no, I just mean he knows how to use the phone... yes, a pay phone....and how to call collect.... Raymond says he left his house to pack some clothes so I'm sure he has clean underwear.... Now, now, there's no need to cry. He'll be alright, he's.... Of course, I don't know for sure how he's doing right this minute but.... Listen, Raymond and I are going to keep on looking.... Yes, we'll call back in about four hours or sooner if we find out something.... Yes, we'll call first thing in the morning or even sooner... No, we won't stop looking.... We will. Bye."

Leon hung up the phone and walked out of the phone booth and loosened his tie. It was a sign of extreme agitation. Maybe he could think more clearly if the tie weren't choking him. Desperate times required desperate measures. He put his hands in his pockets and walked slowly back toward the hearse, then stopped next to the gas pump, his legs spread apart, his eyes looking to the fading night sky. I noted that Miss Jane had not asked and Leon had not told her where we were. For several minutes, he didn't say anything; then he said, "Okay, Raymond. Here's what we're going to do. We're going to go into that station and find out where in the hell we are."

Inside the station there was an older gentleman sitting in a rocking chair beside a tall, red, Coca-Cola vending machine. When we walked in, I believe we woke him from a good sleep. "Hello, gentlemen, what can I do for you?" he asked.

"Need a little help," replied Leon. "We're from Taggart, Virginia, and we seem to have lost our way. We were headed toward Greensboro, but evidently we have not gone in the right direction for the last few hours. Could you give us some direction?"

"Well, mister, I can sure help you some. First of all, you're a long way from Greensboro but not very far from Taggart. Fact is, if you just go out in front of the station here and take a left and don't turn nowhere else, you'll be back in Taggart in 'bout a hour."

"What!!" was the only response Leon could muster.

"Yep. Not but 'bout twenty miles north as the crow flies; but since you gotta drive on them curvy mountain roads, it's near 'bout seventy miles."

Leon just stood there, looking like he was about to cry. Then he said, "I believe I'll have a Pepsi and a pack o' nabs. You want anything, Raymond?" I told him I'd take the same. Leon paid for the items, and we got back in the hearse and turned left in front of the station.

"Not a word. I don't want to hear it," he said flatly as we drove back toward Taggart.

Leon and I hardly talked at all on the way back to Taggart.

When we were almost there, Leon said, "I guess we'll have to go by and tell Jane about our foolhardy trip. I guess we all just wanted so much to go right on out and find Jubal, we didn't really think through anything; we just reacted. First thing in the morning I'm going to go down to the police station and check with Chief Gains and see if he's heard anything from his missing-persons bulletin."

Leon took me home before he went to Miss Jane's house. I guess he didn't want me around to see him admit the foolish and unproductive activity of the day.

Chapter 10

The motor of the old Dodge had settled into a steady hum as it sped into the foothills of North Carolina. All the windows had been rolled down, and the music of Bill Monroe and the Bluegrass Boys struggled through the scratchy static of the radio and the muffling sound of the wind blowing through the car.

Blue moon of Kentucky keep on shining,
Shine on the one that's gone and left me blue…

"We kinda sound like that, don't we, Clement?" asked Curtis.

"Not hardly," was the reply. "'Bout the only thing we got in common with Bill Monroe and his bunch is the instruments we play…and we don't play them near as good as they do."

"Now we ain't all that bad, Clement," said Craven. "When we get everything going right and in tune, we do pretty good. You know people tell us that all the time."

"Oh, yeah. We must be wonderful since we got a show near 'bout every night" was Clement's sarcastic reply.

"The reason we ain't got no more shows is 'cause we ain't got nobody promotin' us," reasoned Curtis. "We wait 'til we get to a town 'fore we ever tell anybody we gon' be playing there; and when we do tell 'em, all they see is a old wore-out-lookin' bunch o' hillbillies. They ain't gon' shell out a dollar to hear us."

"What we need is a sponsor like they got on the Grand Ol' Opry," said Jubal. "All the big-name bands got sponsors. They get 'em on the radio, and they pay for their suits and stuff. All we'd have to do is put the sponsor's name on something so people would associate us with the sponsor."

"Who is 'we'?" asked Clement. "Since when did you become a member of this band?"

"You just said you needed a promoter. Well, that's me. 'Sides that, I'm gonna find us a sponsor soon as we get to someplace besides these empty roads."

It seemed that Jubal had taken on an expanded air of confidence since he had successfully convinced the group of the efficiency of moonshine as automobile fuel and persuaded the station owner to take fake moonshine as payment for real gasoline.

Sometime that night the group decided they needed to pull over and rest and get their bearings. Jubal saw a phone booth at an intersection and told them to pull over there. Jubal went into the phone booth.

"Mama?"

That familiar voice startled Jane Simpson as she answered the phone while preparing a solitary breakfast that morning. Another voice interrupted, "Will you accept this collect call from Jubal?"

"Yes, yes. Jubal? Are you alright? Where are you?" Jane Simpson almost shouted into the phone, her voice worn and raspy from the lack of sleep and her worry about her youngest son.

"I'm okay, Mama. A whole lot has happened but ain't nothin' wrong, and I'm still on my way to catch up with Mac." Jubal could hear the worry in his mother's voice and felt a pang of guilt. For just a moment, he considered going back home.

"Have you had anything to eat? Did you take any clean underwear? I'm so worried, Jubal. Please come on back home, and we'll all go down to see Mac together. You know Mac wouldn't want anything to happen to you."

"Don't worry, Mama. I've run up with some good folks. One of 'em was a preacher so you know God is lookin' after me. He musta been 'cause He sent some other folks, famous musicians, to get me outta the burning tent; and they are taking me with 'em on to Fort Bragg."

"The burning tent? Oh, Jubal, Jubal! Musicians? Transients? You can't trust those kinds of people. You know better than to take up with strangers. You don't know what they might do."

"They're alright, Mama. 'Sides, I'm helping pay my way by helping them promote their shows. I'm pretty sure they'll want to keep me around to help out like that."

"Oh, my! They are holding you in bondage like Joseph in Egypt.

95

Don't let them use you and throw you away, darlin'."

Jubal began to tell his mother all the things he was planning to do, most of which he was thinking up as he spoke. As Jubal began to explain his plans for the band, Jane began to realize that Jubal wasn't going to listen to her pleas to return on his own. She would need to use a subtler approach, find out where he was so that Leon and Raymond could find him. In a much quieter tone, she asked, "What kind of band is this?"

"They play bluegrass. You know, kinda hillbilly country," he replied.

"And do they play in bars? Please don't go into those places. I've heard about those honky tonks; that's what they call them. That's what I hear them singing about on the radio. Drinking and women and..." Jane was about to return to her alarmist tone before she realized that she needed to sound calm if she were to find out where Jubal was doing all the band promotion. "What kind of places do you have them scheduled for?" she asked.

"Well, none right now. But it's not too far to Greensboro and we oughta..." Jubal realized that he had just been trapped into letting his mother know his whereabouts. "Listen, I gotta go, Mama. I'm alright and I love you," he said as he quickly hung up the phone.

Chapter 11

As soon as she hung up the phone, Miss Jane called Leon. "Leon, Jubal called!!! He's alright, but I don't know where he is. He said he was with some traveling band of hillbillies, but he didn't say where they were."

"Well, that's good news. At least we know he's alright. He'll call us again, I'm sure. In the meantime, I'll go down to the police station and bring Chief Gains up-to-date."

After Leon dropped me off at my house, I stood out in the yard a few minutes before I went in. The light in the living room was still on, so I knew that Dad was still up. I was really reluctant to tell him that our trip had not only been nonproductive but also foolish. Fortunately, I had always been able to tell my dad the truth, even when I knew there would be some sort of retribution for my action.

As I went in the front door, Dad was hanging up the telephone. He didn't look surprised to see me. He said, "I figured y'all would be back tonight. Thought it might be a little bit earlier. I was just calling Chief Gains to see if he had heard anything from his missingpersons bulletin or from you and Leon. I guess I need to call him back and tell him you're back here."

I told him about what had happened. He just sorta smiled and said, "Well, I guess it stands to reason that if you keep taking nothing but left turns you just go in circles, particularly on these winding mountain roads. But don't be too hard on yourselves; I didn't think through this thing myself either. I guess I was a lot like you and Leon; I just saw how upset Jane was and wanted to help her, and she was telling us what to do so we did it. Nothing wrong with that. Now we have to give the situation a little more thought. I'll go see Chief Gains in the morning, and we'll assess the situation without getting everybody's emotions involved. Go on to bed now. Get a good night's sleep and we'll start over in the morning."

The next morning Dad let me go with him down to the police station.

The Taggart police station, town hall and fire station were and still are all in one building. The fire station is on the west end with two open bays and a fire truck in each bay. The town manager, tax and maintenance departments have offices on the other end, and the police station is in the middle. All the town maintenance equipment is behind the building in a fenced-in yard that stays muddy all year because there's a busted water line under it that resists an almost-continuous repair effort.

Chief Raeford Gains had been the chief of police for as long as I could remember. He had only three deputies and a dispatcher to help him maintain law and order in Taggart, and they did a good job. Fortunately, there was not a lot of crime to deal with in Taggart.

The chief greeted them, "Good mornin', Mr. Lovejoy. You too, Raymond."

"Morning to you, Chief," responded my dad. "Anything come back about Jubal Simpson?"

"No, sir. After you called last night, I checked all our wire services and didn't see a thing. I don't know what to tell you at this point. Without any idea of where he was headed—other than Fort Bragg—I don't know how we can go looking for him. Bad as it sounds, 'bout all we can do right now is wait."

"Well, Jane's not going to want to hear that, but I know you're right."

Jubal stood in the phone booth with his hand still on the receiver and looked out through the dirty glass walls around him at the little crossroads where he and the band had spent the night. There was a sign where two roads intersected that said "Prince Albert." Jubal didn't know if they were in Virginia or North Carolina; he just knew that he was not in Taggart, and he was probably a little closer to Fort Bragg.

They had stopped at that particular crossroad because they had all decided that they needed to stop somewhere, get some sleep and find out where they were. Each had taken a turn driving; but when it came time for Clement to drive, he proposed they stop somewhere and reassess their situation. When Jubal saw the phone booth, he told Clement to stop right there. He needed to call his mama.

There was a picnic table placed under some trees a few feet from the telephone booth, and the band members were sitting around the table in a bleary daze when Jubal joined them.

"Well, you figured out where we are, Clement?" asked Milford.

"Sign says 'Prince Albert,'" was the reply.

"Yes, sir, that narrows it right down, don't it? Why don't we ask some of the residents that live behind that signpost where their town is?" asked Milford sarcastically.

"It's for sure we ain't gonna get our bearings from here, and I bet we ain't got enough gas to just go lookin' down whichever road," added Curtis.

"We could split up, and one of us go down each road from here," suggested Clement.

"You mean walkin'?" exclaimed Milford.

"Unless you got a mule in your pocket, yeah," replied Clement.

"Well, I ain't had a bite to eat now in near 'bout two days. 'Less somebody's got some food on 'em, I'm goin' to start walkin' 'til I find something, even if it's road kill," said Curtis as he started walking down the dirt road.

Dark clouds had kept the sun from bringing much light to the morning. As the group lamented their situation, a few drops of rain began to fall; then a distant sound of thunder caused all their faces to look skyward as they ran toward their car.

Once inside the car, they all sat in silence as the sound of the rain falling on the car got louder. The coolness of the morning air pressed against the car, causing the windows to fog up. No one inside the car moved, not even to clear the windows. Finally Jubal asked, "How much gas you reckon we got, Milford?"

Milford turned on the engine so the gas gauge would work. "Oh, not much. The needle's just about down to the E."

"Don't y'all reckon we would have a better chance of finding something or somebody if we were going in one direction or the other instead of just sittin' here?" Jubal asked.

"You're right, boy," Milford replied as he cleared off a spot of fog from the windshield, shifted the car into reverse and started to back out onto the dirt road they had been on. Suddenly the car jarred to a stop with a thud that meant they had hit something more solid than their car.

"What the hell was that?" exclaimed Clement as he tried to look out the rear window while wiping away some of the clinging moisture. "I can't see nothin'," he said as he turned to open the rear door. As he did so, the door was jerked open, a gust of wind blew the rain into the car and Clement would have been soaked if the rain had not been blocked by the biggest man he had ever seen.

The man was well over six-feet tall. His bib overalls and flannel shirt covered a body so wide Clement could not see around him through the door frame of the car. He wore an old, tattered, wide-brimmed felt hat that provided little protection from the pouring

101

rain. Under the hat was a face so black, the features of his face were almost indistinguishable.

"You gentlemen need to follow me before you drown," the man said. Then he turned and began walking down a small path that led through the woods past where the picnic table was.

"Follow him," instructed Clement.

"What?" exclaimed Milford. "We don't know him or where he's goin'! And that path ain't as wide as this car."

"Well, he ain't lost and we are. If that path is wide enough for him to get through, it's wide enough for this car. 'Sides, you wanna get out and argue with him?"

Jubal sat in the back seat of the car and contemplated the scene. He saw a giant black man on foot in the pouring rain leading a carload of white men up a gradually-rising path through the woods to an unknown destination. And the car had a case with a bass fiddle in it tied to the top of the car.

Jubal didn't know exactly where he was; but he did know, in a lot of ways, that he was a long way from Taggart, Virginia.

After a while, the path left the woods and led between rows of tall green corn. As Jubal looked past the expedition leader, he could see a small unpainted house. As they approached the house, the path divided, one path going to a barn and a hog pen and the other toward another stand of woods much like they had just passed through.

The black man walked up to the porch of the house before he

turned and waved for the occupants of the car to join him. It was still raining, but Clement told them all to go on even as lightning reflected off the dark clouds and thunder rolled softly, fading languidly behind them.

"Welcome to my humble home, gentlemen. I'm Albert Watson. I must apologize for frightening you when I pounded on the trunk of your car, but you were about to back into me. I saw your car as I was trying to chase some pigs back into the pen from which they had escaped last night. That crossroad is a very dangerous place to be during a heavy rain since it is at the bottom of conjoining hillsides and subject to flash flooding. You may have been caught in the rushing water."

The group on the porch did not respond. They looked at their host with astonishment, unable to decide who this man was. He was different from anybody they had ever seen, particularly so since he was a black man. They didn't know what to say.

Finally Jubal blurted out as he offered to shake his host's hand, "How do you do, Mr. Watson. I'm Jubal Simpson and these are my friends Clement, Curtis, Melford and Craven. We're a famous bluegrass band on our way to an engagement, and we seem to have lost our way. We appreciate you helping us out."

"Well, I'm glad to be of some assistance, young man. I offer you the hospitality of my home, modest as it is."

"You got anything to eat?" asked Curtis, who then immediately apologized. "I'm sorry, I didn't mean to be rude; it's just that we ain't had nothin' to eat for quite a while."

"I understand. Unfortunately, I don't have much to offer, but we'll see if I can prepare some sort of repast that will stave off the pangs of hunger for a while," was the response.

With that, the man opened the door to the cabin and ushered his guests inside. Once inside the one-room house, Jubal sensed that the building was much more spacious than it appeared from the outside. There was a large table with a white tablecloth next to a wood stove already filled with burning wood. The table was set with simple but elegant plates, silverware and wineglasses. A large oriental carpet covered most of the weathered wooden floor. A canopied bed sat at the other end of the room. On one side of the bed was a chest of drawers and on the other was a grand ebony piano.

The guests stared, fascinated by the incongruity of the scene, their voices muted by the sight of such strangeness.

Albert's voice startled them out of their daze, "Ah, here we are, gentlemen. I hope you enjoy my modest effort. I happen to love cornbread and smoked ham. And that is pure spring water in your glasses, an unmatched vintage, I might add."

The guests sat down at the table and immediately began to eat; their hunger overwhelming their amazement and curiosity.

Albert moved over to the piano as he spoke. "I hope you don't mind if I provide a little musical accompaniment for your dining pleasure. I seldom have guests so I don't have an opportunity to entertain very often."

Still clad in his wet clothing, water dripping from the old hat, Albert began to play. His fingers flew lightly over the keyboard, creating a lilting melody, then changing to sonorous chords that transformed the cabin into a majestic music hall.

The music and the food cast a spell on the travelers. Before they knew it, and without any invitation, they were stretched out on the beautiful carpet and fast asleep.

The next morning, they awoke in a barren room: no table, no chairs, no bed, no stove and no piano. On the floor next to the door was a note in a beautiful swirling script:

Gentlemen, I hope you slept well. Thank you for your visit.
Follow the path through the pine woods. It will take you to town.
Your humble servant, Albert Watson.

The town of Longview existed at the end of the dirt road that emerged from the piney woods. Jubal wondered why a town, even one as small as Longview, would not have a thoroughfare. The road in was also the road out. Small, well-cared-for houses, a grocery store, a barber shop and beauty shop, a gas station/garage and a bank lined the sides of the street. At the end of the street was a small, white, wooden church, its steeple more like a castle parapet than a spire. The road ended in a circular parking lot in front of the church.

A sign placed on a brick base in front of the church said, "Longview Community Church. Welcome. I am the Alpha and the Omega."

Milford made the circle through the parking lot and began to go back up the street. He knew they needed gasoline so he pulled up to the pump at the gas station. Slowly the car came to a halt. There was no movement to be seen. From somewhere in the station came the sound of a radio playing country music. When it seemed that no one was there to serve them, the occupants of the car emerged to look for an attendant.

"Anybody here?" shouted Craven.

"Sure is," came a voice from the garage area. "Whatcha need?" A tall, lanky man dressed in bib overalls came around the corner smiling and wiping his hands on an oily rag.

"Need a little gas. But…" Clement stopped to think how he was going to ask for gas when they had no money.

"But you got no money," observed the attendant.

There was an awkward silence following that exchange. Jubal suddenly proclaimed, "We can make some money to pay for the gas if you'll give us a chance. I noticed there's not a lot going on here, and we are a famous bluegrass band. We could put on a dance here for the town, and you could charge 'em to come."

Another extended silence. Then the man said, his face

expressionless, "Bluegrass music. Hillbilly music. Like that playing on the radio in there?"

"Yes, sir," replied Jubal. "Fact is, you probably heard us on that very radio. We have played on the Grand Ole Opry many times. And Louisiana Hayride. And Lester Flatt and Earl Scruggs used to travel with us too... and Hank Williams is a personal friend of ours. Yes, sir, all you gotta do is let folks know we're in town, and you'll make more than enough to pay for a tank of gas."

Again the service station attendant didn't respond. He just looked over toward the little church and said, "Live music in Longview. Hmm. Now, that'd be something, wouldn't it? Real music. The only live music we ever get around here is that organ down at the church, and I'm so tired of hearing the same old hymns I could near 'bout holler out a yodel just to hear something different." Another pause. "Tell you what, young feller, when I knock off tonight, ya'll set up right here in front of the gas pump and play. I don't care how good or bad you play, it'll be better than that organ stuff, and I'll consider the gas bill settled. That a deal?"

"Yes, sir, that's a deal," said Jubal as he shook hands with the attendant.

"By the way, my name's Virgil Allman," said the band's newest employer.

"Can we go ahead and fill up the tank?" asked Clement.

"I don't think that'd be good business. Why, you might just up and go on outta here if I was to put gas in your car before you play. Y'all just make yourself to home 'til I finish up. Help yourself to a Pepsi and some crackers." Virgil was a practical businessman.

After they had gotten a soft drink and a snack, the band sat themselves down on the shady side of the station under an old sweetgum tree. There was no table, nor even a bench, so they sat on the ground.

"You know that deal ain't legal," said Clement to Jubal. "I'm the manager of this bunch, and I ain't agreed to nothing."

"You got a better idea?" asked Jubal.

"Naw, I guess not. 'Sides, if you can get us more gigs, we might even take you on permanent, eh, boys?" said Clement.

"Well, yeah, we could use a promoter," said Craven. "But now, I don't know 'bout some of his methods. We might not ought to be telling people we played on the Grand Ole Opry and all that stuff. That ain't exactly honest."

"I bet nobody here has ever been to The Grand Ole Opry live, and we sound just as good as anybody that has played on there. 'Specially if all they've heard is organ music," was Jubal's defensive reply. "'Sides, you know I'm just gonna be with y'all 'til I can get to Fort Bragg. Then you're on your own."

Night came to Longview like everything else in that town—very slowly. Somehow during the afternoon, word had spread that there was going to be a band playing in front of Virgil's gas station probably right after supper. By the time Virgil turned on the lights over the gas pump, several people had gathered on the street and around the station. Some sat in folding chairs. (Jubal thought it worth noting that some of the folding metal chairs had "Longview Community Church" stamped on the back of them.) Others brought wooden chairs that had just been under the supper table in their kitchen, and some just leaned against their cars parked randomly in front of the station.

When it got dark enough that the light formed a border that indicated a temporary stage, Clement and the other band members took their places. Jubal, the erstwhile manager, assumed a position on the edge of the street where he could observe both the band and the audience.

It was an eclectic repertoire that ranged from traditional folk songs to some gospel favorites, all played with vigor and sung in a high-pitched harmony. "Uncle Pen," "Peach Picking in Georgia,"

"Rollin' in My Sweet Baby's Arms," mixed in with "I'm Using My Bible for a Road Map" and "Victory in Jesus." But when they got to "Salty Dog Blues," the small crowd began to join in the expression of the music. An older couple began to dance what could have been clogging, or it could have been square dance steps or it could have all been improvised. Whatever it was, it was energetic and contagious.

Let me be your salty dog,

Or I won't be your dog at all.
Honey, let me be your salty dog.

As the music rang through the night, the people of Longview celebrated. They danced and sang along with the band. They applauded and shouted their approval; and when Clement announced they would be playing the final selection, they shouted for more.

Jubal looked at the assembly with awe. He had never seen people so excited, so moved by music that they were swept up and transported to some ecstatic level of consciousness.

Clement attempted to end the evening by introducing each song as the last one, but each time the crowd called for more. The musicians were beginning to get very tired; they had been playing continuously for nearly three hours. Finally, Clement said, "That's it, folks; there just ain't no more."

Virgil walked up before the crowd and said, "They done what they said, folks. Now, I gotta live up to my part of the deal. Y'all just go on home." Then he turned to Clement and said, "I'll go ahead and fill up your gas tank. You done good."

Virgil turned the handle on the side of the gas pump, removed the nozzle and took the cap off the car's gas tank. Suddenly a man who had been laughing and dancing just moments before ran up to Virgil and jerked the nozzle from his hand. "Not yet," he shouted to

Virgil. "They got to play some more."

Virgil was so startled he couldn't react so he just stared at the man as the crowd chanted, "More! More! More!"

The lady who had started the dancing came up to Clement and said, "Play somethin' pretty, mister!" to which Clement replied, "Lady, we can't play no more. We're give out."

"Play anyway!" she shouted as she grabbed Clement's collar.

As Jubal looked around, he saw that each of the band members had been accosted by one of the villagers. Since they didn't know he was associated with the group, no one had approached him. But just as he started to try to rescue somebody—anybody—he heard a feminine voice scream in his ear, "Come on!! Get behind me!"

He turned to find a girl mounted on a horse. The horse and rider were remarkably calm amid all the chaos. "Come on before it really gets rowdy!" she said as she motioned for Jubal to get up behind her on the horse.

The girl reached down and took Jubal's arm, simultaneously kicking the horse. Jubal was pulled up by the force of the action, and the pair sped past the crowd down the only street in town into the darkness.

They didn't ride very far before the girl pulled the horse down to a walk. "No need running too far; they aren't going to follow us," she said. "They didn't even notice us leaving town, and nobody ever leaves town anyway."

Jubal was so overcome by all that had just taken place that he couldn't speak. He ran the scene through his mind, trying to assess what was real and what was unreal. It all began so simply: a quiet, boring afternoon waiting to play in exchange for the gasoline, the silence bearing down on them like the hot sun as the group dozed in the shade of the gum tree. Then the excited crowd. From there it was a blur. Now he was seated behind a beautiful girl mounted on a horse and riding through the night. He had his arms wrapped tightly around the girl's waist, his body pushed close to hers. Not even a saddle separated the two. He could feel their bodies move together with each step the horse took into the night, the only sound the soft sound of the horse's hooves striking the road. Her hair blew into his face, the smell like fresh lemons.

He finally voiced his confusion when he asked the girl, "What happened back there and who are you?"

"My name's Jenny, Jenny Balieu. I'm going to put you off right here; then I'm going to head on back to town." She stopped the horse and said, "Get down."

Jubal swung his leg over the back of the horse and dropped to the ground. As the girl turned the horse back toward the town, she said, "You just keep walking down this road 'til you get to the fork, then turn right and that'll take you back out to the main highway."

"Wait, wait!" pleaded Jubal. "Don't just leave me out here. At least tell me what happened back there."

Jenny stopped the horse, her back still to Jubal. "It's probably best that you don't know. If you told anybody, they wouldn't believe you anyway."

"Please, please don't go. Just stay here a while 'til I get my bearings."

The girl didn't immediately respond to Jubal's plea; but after a few more moments of consideration, she swung her right leg over the neck of the horse and dismounted nimbly.

"Alright, Mr. Jubal Simpson, I'll tell you what you want to know."

Leading the horse, she began walking down the middle of the road. It wasn't really much of a road anymore, just two worn parallel paths, the median between them covered with weeds. Jubal followed her.

"How'd you know my name?" Jubal asked.

"Prince Albert told me," she replied. "He told me he was sending you into town after you spent the night at his cabin. Wanted me to look out for you. He figured something like this might happen."

"Well, if you can tell me what happened, I'd sure appreciate it.

I don't believe I have ever seen people so wrought up before. It's like they were possessed."

"In a way that's exactly what happened. You see, Longview doesn't have many visitors. Nobody ever goes there on purpose, and nobody ever leaves 'cause they've got nowhere to go and no reason to go there. Everything just is. So life just kinda exists 'til something or somebody comes along and provides some stimulation.

"When you and your band arrived, everybody in town knew about it. They saw you drive down the street and around the parking lot at the church and over to the gas station. They knew Virgil got you to stay and play in exchange for gasoline. They knew you had a soft drink and crackers. All that was the most excitement they had experienced in a long time. So when you began to play, the music was an accelerant; it created an energy so strong and so new to the people that they became over-stimulated, like they had gotten some sort of drug injected into their spirit.

"Prince Albert says that the human body will only exist if the spirit will support it. He says that music is the greatest stimulation for the human spirit. The music the band created took over the spirit of the people of Longview just as much as a drug takes over the body and mind; and when the music stopped, it was just like going through withdrawal from a drug addiction. Those people would have done anything to hear more music. Music speaks to the good in people, and the withdrawal speaks to the bad. And that's what happened back there, Jubal Simpson. That town was going through withdrawal, a withdrawal of the human spirit, an under-nourished spirit that had been over-stimulated by music."

As they traveled down the weed-covered road, Jubal had

overtaken Jenny, walking beside her as the horse followed. The trio passed through the woods as the moon shown through the trees, and the stars poked little pinholes in the sky, letting in light from the universe beyond. For a while they walked that way in silence, Jubal trying to absorb all Jenny had told him. Then abruptly Jubal stopped and looked around them. They had come up to an intersection that looked familiar even in the moonlight. It was the same intersection where he and the band had spent the night. The sign that indicated it was "Prince Albert" still stood in one corner, the telephone booth in the other.

"Hey," he said, "This is where we stopped the other night!"

"Yes," said Jenny, "and this is where I'll leave you. Follow the same road you came in on, then go south at the next paved road."

"But wait. Don't leave me here. You still haven't told me why you weren't affected like the other townspeople."

Jenny walked over to the picnic table, tied the horse to the pine tree next to it, then sat on the top of the picnic table. "I didn't get over-stimulated like the others because I play music every day. Prince Albert taught me to play the piano, but nobody knows about it. He comes by every once in a while and gives me lessons. When he came for a lesson yesterday, he told me you were coming."

"This Prince Albert, he's Albert Watson, the man who took us to his cabin and played the piano? He's kind of a peculiar fellow. Talks a lot different from what he looks, and his house is weird.

115

Who is he?"

"I wouldn't call him *peculiar* exactly; *unique* might be a better word. He told me he had studied music in Europe and played concerts all over the world. Said he used to accompany a fellow named Paul Robeson who was a famous singer. I never heard of either one of them."

"Is he a real prince?" asked Jubal.

"Of course. I'm a prince if I say I am. The reality, however, might be a matter of viewpoint," came a voice from the woods behind the picnic table. Albert Watson emerged from the same wooded path down which he had led Jubal and his friends earlier.

The sound and sight of the man had startled Jubal and Jenny even as the horse stood calmly where he was tethered. Jenny had jumped up from the table and was standing beside Jubal as if he could now rescue her. But they both quickly calmed as they recognized the giant figure before them.

Albert Watson stood wrapped in a black cape which flowed behind him when he moved forward, revealing a white, ruffled shirt above a pair of dark brown pants, the legs of which were stuffed into knee-high black boots. *Majestic, even noble,* thought Jubal.

"My father said I was a prince. That's why he placed that sign here. This is the place where my coronation took place. There was no ceremony, no crowning, just my father making the declaration. That was all the confirmation I needed; and, as far as my father and

I were concerned, that is all that was needed. We are who we are because we believe in ourselves, not what someone else believes. Remember that, Jubal Simpson and Jenny Balieu."

And with his words hanging in the night air, the mysterious Prince Albert Watson strolled back into the woods as quietly as he had emerged from them.

Jubal and Jenny stood staring after the man. Was he real? How did he come and go like that? They stood together looking into the woods for a long time. Each had instinctively reached for the other's hand when the prince had startled them. They slowly unclasped their hands as they realized the physical connection. But there remained another connection they could not identify, something that seemed to join them together, something they now shared that eluded them before. Maybe it was because the prince had addressed them as a couple, a unit, when just a few minutes earlier they had been two very different individuals.

Jubal was confused. He wanted to leave that place, to get on with the search for his brother. He even thought maybe he ought to go on back home. Given all that had happened to him since he left Taggart, he was a little afraid of what might lie ahead. But he wanted to stay there too, right there with this girl who had sprung into his life unannounced and unexpected, a beautiful girl who had saved him from the raging crowd and spirited him away and made him feel…. He didn't know what he felt or what to do about it.

Jenny was the first to speak. "I'll go with you," she said as if she was reading his thoughts.

Her words jarred Jubal from his reverie. "What? Are you crazy? You don't even know me or where I'm going. I don't even know where to go from here to get to where I think I want to go!"

"It doesn't matter. I can't go back to Longview. I realized a long time ago I would have to leave there to literally go out into the real world. Now is the time," she said.

"How 'bout your family? They'll worry about you, come looking for you."

"There is no family. There's just me."

"What do you mean, 'no family'? How do you live?"

"Longview is a place that just is, and I just was…and now I'm here," was her reply.

And so it was that Jenny and Jubal started on a journey together, a continuing odyssey for Jubal and a new life for Jenny. As they rode out of Prince Albert the Place that night, Jubal sitting behind Jenny on the horse, she asked, "Where are we going?"

"Ahead," replied Jubal.

Chapter 12

As they rode down the poorly-defined road through the woods, Jenny and Jubal assessed their situation. The first thing they realized was that with all the excitement, they had not slept, nor had they eaten anything; and they had no money nor even a change of clothes, pretty practical considerations that had not been a concern when placed in the context of Prince Albert's philosophical utterances. Usually, when practicality challenges philosophy in the face of reality, practicality wins.

For good or bad, the hunger kept them from falling asleep as the steady walking gait of the horse tempted Morpheus to sweep them up. It may have just been their youthful constitution that kept them going, but the need for food and rest went on unabated as they passed on down the road. Even when the road opened up and wide fields of corn replaced the trees, no habitation came in sight. When they eventually came to a paved road as the sun began to rise, there was still nothing to encourage them.

Jubal looked toward the sun as it rose above the cornfield and watched it slowly spread its glow like a giant candle pushing the night away.

Suddenly the two riders heard what seemed a foreign sound. A car was coming up behind them. They turned to watch its approach even as the horse continued his somnambulistic trek down the shoulder of the road. As the car drew closer and the sun more illuminative, they could see that it was a police car, its big light on the top of the car, the words SHERIFF printed on the front. Then for some unexplainable reason, the driver of the car turned on the flashing light and just bumped the siren. After the long hours of silence, any noise would have been, at the least, startling; but a police siren combined with a bright light flashing in the dawn's dim glow panicked the horse. The plodding pony, who had so resolutely and comfortably carried his passengers through the night, became as wild and uncontrollable as an untamed mustang, his hooves beating a wild accompaniment on the pavement. Jenny pulled on the reins with no result as Jubal clung to Jenny.

The police car was in pursuit, the red light flashing and siren wailing. When the car drew up beside the panicked horse, the driver of the car shouted out to Jenny, "Pull over!"

Jenny had realized the futility of trying to stop the horse and was just trying to stay on and anticipate where her steed was taking her. Jubal just held on to Jenny. As they rounded a sharp curve in the road, the horse decided to continue in a straight course and proceeded to jump the ditch that ran between the road and the cornfield. He was successful in the effort; but when he continued to run down through the cornfield, he was unencumbered by his previous passengers. Jenny lay in the edge of the cornfield, broken cornstalks pushed to the ground around her but unhurt. Jubal lay on the ditch bank at the edge of the field. Jenny quickly gathered herself together and rushed over to him.

"Are you alright?" she asked anxiously.

"Yeah, I think so. Kinda knocked the wind outta me for a minute," he replied. But he had not escaped the mud of the ditch bank. He was covered with black, sticky mud that coated his clothes and clung to his hair and face. "My best shirt, too," he said gloomily.

"And your only one," said Jenny. Then they both laughed at the absurdity of their situation as Jenny tried to pull some of the mud from Jubal's hair and brush the same from his face.

As they were standing there in the field, the sheriff's car returned and pulled over to the side of the road, the ditch bank between the car and the stranded and muddy couple. The light atop the car was still flashing. The man who emerged from the car was tall and thin and wore a khaki uniform with a deputy sheriff's badge attached to his shirt. A thin black tie was loosely tied around his neck, and his official peaked cap rested on the back of his head. But the most notable point on his visage was a thick, grey mustache.

After he got out of the car, he stood with his hands on his hips looking over at the couple on the other side of the ditch bank. "Y'all alright?" he shouted although he was only a few feet away.

Jenny declared herself the spokesman for the two by asserting in a voice that pierced the morning air, "No, we're not okay! We're sore and muddy and hungry and tired and…and it's your fault! Only a non-thinking ignoramus would do what you did! Did you think any living animal or human would just come to a halt when you did what you did? Now you have not only put us in this condition but deprived us of our transportation!" Then she began to cry.

Jubal stood beside Jenny as she proceeded through her tirade. He wondered if this were the same girl who had rescued him from the crowd and joined him in his journey, courageously casting her lot with his? Was this the stoically philosophical Joan of Arc who had guided them out of the woods in the dark of night? He looked at her wondering what he should do; after all, he was the man, who should be her protector. Then he noticed that not a single tear fell from her eyes.

The dumfounded deputy didn't know how to respond. "Well, I… uh uh…was…just…uh. Missy, I didn't mean you no harm. I was just lettin' you know I was there so your horse wouldn't jump out in front of me. I didn't know he was some wild…"

"Wild? Wild? I have raised that horse from a colt. He's the calmest, most gentle horse in the world. But you couldn't imagine that, could you? You just wanted to make yourself known to the world, to inflict yourself on two hapless and helpless young people struggling on the road of life." Jenny quickly turned and hugged Jubal, placing her head on his shoulder as she whispered, "Did I go too far?"

Jubal seized that moment to speak before the deputy could process Jenny's histrionics. "Officer, I didn't know we broke any laws or anything like that. We were just going on our way to find my brother who's joined the army down at Fort Bragg."

"Fort Bragg? Why, son, that's a long ways from here, and you ain't even headed that way. You near 'bout to Greensboro but you're headed west. You need to be going the other way. Besides, you're not going to make it on a horse anyway." The deputy paused to consider the next move as he stroked his big mustache, pushing it down around his mouth. "Tell ya what I'll do. I'll make this all up to you. Y'all get in the car and I'll drive you to somewhere where you can get cleaned up, and I'll getcha something to eat... and then... I don't know. We'll figure something out."

So Jubal and Jenny got in the deputy's car, and they headed on down the road in the opposite direction they had been riding on the horse.

They rode in silence for a while; then the deputy asked, "You really think you were goin' to ride that horse all the way to Fort Bragg?"

"Uh, no, sir. Probably not. There's a lot of things about this trip we haven't worked out yet," answered Jubal. "Lots of things."

"Well, I can understand that. Travel nowadays is a complicated process. Takes a lot of plannin'. Now take my trip to my family reunion last year. Why it took me near 'bout all day to get from my house in Reidsville down to Sanford. 'Course all that fried chicken and stuff my wife fixed smelled so good I had to eat on it while I was driving, and that cut down on my driving time considerable. You know, fried chicken'll fill up your mind as well as your belly if you don't watch out."

Nobody said anything else until they had gone about twenty miles; then the deputy turned onto a small farm road marked at the highway by a large mailbox with "Sykes 109" stenciled on the side.

"Gonna take you by Mama's," was all the deputy said.

Mama's was a small frame house with a fresh coat of purple paint and a roof covered with rusty tin; the edges, tenuously attached at the front corners, flapped in the morning breeze. Behind the house were some small outbuildings and a large barn and behind them a big field of green tobacco, the broad leaves overlapping in the long rows.

There was a woman sitting in a rocking chair on the short porch that jutted out from the house. As she watched the deputy's car drive up in her yard, she continued rocking in the chair; a wisp of smoke drifted up from the cigarette she held between her fingers.

"Y'all come on and meet Mama," the deputy instructed as he got out of the car. Jubal and Jenny dutifully followed him up to the foot of the wooden steps that led up to the porch. The woman on the porch continued to rock as she silently surveyed the trio before her.

She was a small, tidy woman. Her gray hair tied in a bun came barely to the top of the back of the rocking chair. She wore a red print dress covered with a clean white apron, and on her feet she wore thin white socks stuffed into a pair of tan sandals.

The deputy began to introduce Jubal and Jenny to his mother. "Mama, this is …. Well, I messed up again. I don't even know your names," he said apologetically to Jubal and Jenny.

"My name's Jubal and this is my friend Jenny," said Jubal, trying to diminish the deputy's embarrassment.

"Well, I'm pleased to meet you both," responded the woman as she continued to rock in her chair. "I'm Maybelle Sikes, Marvin Lee's mama, even though I sometimes wonder if I ought to claim him."

"They had a little problem out on the road there; and I thought you might could help 'em get straightened out so they can get on down to Fort Bragg," interjected Marvin Lee.

"Uh, huh. Well, I tell you what, y'all do look a sight; and I don't expect you got a lotta choice right now about what you gonna do. Are they in trouble with the law, Marvin Lee?"

"No, ma'am. They just had some bad luck is all. It's kinda my fault. I don't want to have to take 'em into town 'cause I'll have to explain everything to Sheriff Tate, and I'd just as soon not do that."

"I figured you had messed up somehow when you pulled up here with them in the back seat," she said accusingly as she took a draw from the cigarette. "And you knowed I'd take care of 'em, didn't you? Well, 'course I will. You need to keep your job, and they need to get on down the road. I can help both situations, I reckon." As she got up slowly from her chair, she said, "You young'uns come on in the house here, and we'll do what we need to do." As she flipped the remainder of the cigarette into the yard, she said, "Marvin Lee, you come back and get 'em in the mornin'."

As Marvin Lee got back in the patrol car, Maybelle took a stern look at her new charges. "Just wait a minute. We might not oughta go in the house with all that mud and stuff on ya. Humm. I expect Jenny oughta go on to the back porch and get shed of them clothes and you do the same right here, Jubal. Ain't nobody gonna see you this far from the road. Here, put this apron around you when you get naked; then I'll come and get you when Jenny gets decent."

Jubal did as he was instructed, then sat down in the rocking chair with only the apron wrapped around him. He sat there for quite a while before Maybelle came to the front door and said, "Alright, get on in here and let's see if we can make you look any better."

Maybelle led him through a small living room and down a narrow, short hallway before she pointed out the bathroom at the end of the hall. She said, "I ain't got but the one bathroom, and Jenny done used up most of the hot water so you do the best you can in there. There's a towel and washcloth on the side of the tub. Call me when you get through, and I'll bring something for you to put on." She closed the door and left Jubal standing in the bathroom in her apron.

After a brief ablution, Jubal called out, "Miss Maybelle, I'm done!" He waited a minute with no response so he shouted out again, "Miss Maybelle, I'm through washing up!" The bathroom door opened up, and a pair of pants and a shirt were tossed into the room.

From the hallway Maybelle expounded, "That's all I can find right now. Ain't no man lived here goin' on ten years so I couldn't find nothin' right away. Them's my late husband's. You just have to do without any drawers 'til I can wash them you had on."

Jubal picked the pants up and held them at arm's length. *Mr. Sykes must have been a big man,* he said to himself, then proceeded to put on the khaki pants that would have fit a man three times Jubal's size. The shirt, a long-sleeve denim was equally spacious, but he could roll up the sleeves. He couldn't take in the waist of the pants, however, so he exited the bathroom holding the pants up with one hand as he walked down the hallway and through a door that led to the kitchen. And there was Jenny. And Maybelle and a stove and refrigerator and some other stuff. But Jubal only saw Jenny. She was wearing a print dress much like the one Maybelle wore, but she looked much different. Her dark hair was still wet and pulled back and tied with a blue ribbon and, like Jubal, she wore no shoes.

"Hey," she said with a smile as she continued spreading peanut butter on a piece of white bread.

It had been only a couple of hours since they had arrived at the house, but it seemed to Jubal like a lifetime ago since he had heard Jenny's voice or seen her. Now here she was looking so different from the ranting, muddy combatant he had stood beside on the ditch bank earlier that very morning. He was speechless.

"Here," said Maybelle as she opened a kitchen drawer and withdrew an electrical extension cord and handed it to Jubal. "You better tie this around them pants 'fore your mind completely leaves you and you forget to hold 'em up. There's peanut butter and jelly and bread over there. Go ahead and fix yourself a sandwich and get some of that iced tea. That ought to hold you 'til I can fix us a proper supper," she continued. She turned her back to the sink and leaned against it as she explained all that she had to do. "I got y'all's clothes in the washing machine out on the back porch. If it don't rain, I'll hang 'em on the line this afternoon. I got a lot to do. I gotta check on that barn full of tobacco out there. It'll cure out tonight, and we can take it out of the barn in the mornin' so we can put another one in tomorrow. Them leaves gotta come off the stalk in this heat. We gotta get it 'fore the sun burns it up in the field. Lord knows it's gonna be hot work! That dry tobacco in the barn won't hardly be cooled off when we climb up in there to get it; and croppin' them green leaves in the field with the sun beatin' down on you... well, it's just a hard way to make a living, I tell ya, but that's what we gotta do."

When Maybelle stopped talking, there was an awkward silence

in the kitchen. She had expected at least a question about tobacco, but none was forthcoming. Jubal and Jenny had taken their sandwiches and iced tea to the table and were looking at the food intently as they ate.

"Y'all ain't heard nothin' I said, have ya?" asked Maybelle. She took a cigarette out of a pack of Camels and lit it, took a puff, propped one elbow in the opposite hand and said, "This is gonna be a interesting visit."

After his lunch, Jubal decided he needed to be alone for just a little while to sort through all the things that had happened since he had left Taggart just a few days earlier. All he wanted to do was catch up with his brother so they could go fight in a war just like his ancestors had gone off together to fight the Yankees. He had not anticipated that the effort to follow that family tradition would be such a complicated task.

Mid-summer afternoons in central North Carolina tend to be hot and muggy. Even where the land might roll a little bit, it is too far from the mountains or the ocean for any breeze to cool the air; so, as the afternoon passed, the heat just sagged around the shade of the pecan trees that loomed between Maybelle's house and the barns.

He meandered past the clothesline where his and Jenny's clothes were still soaking wet, then on toward the tobacco field. He walked in a wilted silence, the heat so stifling that even the birds were muted.

The over-sized shirt and pants became heavier as the sweat from his body soaked the cloth. As he looked out over the tobacco field, he recalled how he had heard about how hot it was to work in those fields. He had never done it himself, but he had heard the tobacco farmers that came into the hardware store and some of the older boys at school talk about it. Maybelle had said they would need to be in the fields the next day. He wondered if "they" meant him. *I really need to get on to Fort Bragg,* he thought.

He turned back toward the house as he heard the sound of a car coming up the dirt driveway, dust blossoming behind it. It was Marvin Lee's patrol car, and Jubal wondered what would bring the deputy back out to his mother's so soon. He saw Marvin Lee get out of the car and run into the house. His curiosity overcoming the heat, Jubal held on to the waistband of his baggy pants as he ran toward the house.

The screen door slammed behind him as he rushed into the house, on through the kitchen and into the small living room. Maybelle had placed a window fan in the side window of the living room, and its artificial breeze greeted Jubal as he entered the room.

"It means I gotta take 'em in, Mama," Marvin Lee said as Jubal entered the room. "That's my duty."

"Let me think on this a minute, boy," said Maybelle.

"What's the matter?" asked Jubal of anybody.

"Marvin Lee says there's a missing-person bulletin out for you," answered Jenny.

Marvin Lee looked at Jubal as he said, "The sheriff showed it to all of us when I got back to the office. I didn't tell him I'd seen y'all, but I gotta take you in anyway. That's my sworn duty as an officer of the law. Evidently your mama wants you to come home. It didn't say whether you'd been kidnapped or just run away from home. Either way, I gotta take you in."

Jubal wasn't surprised that his mother had gotten the law involved in looking for him. He knew she would be worried; that's why he had called her to let her know he was alright. But he also knew that all mamas worry about their children when they're not looking directly at them.

"What about Jenny?" asked Jubal.

"Weren't no mention of her," replied Marvin Lee.

"Alright now, everybody sit down," said Maybelle as she sat down on the tattered blue couch, pulled out a fresh Camel and lit it.

"We going to talk about this thing. Now, Jenny's been telling me a little bit about this trip y'all on and how y'all got together and all. I ain't 'bout to say I understand how everything's come about, but we need to do some considerin' here. First thing we got to consider is your mama, Jubal. You know she's worried near 'bout to death 'bout you. So we got to let her know you're here and you're okay. I don't know exactly how we can apply that consideration to you, Jenny, but we'll study on that later."

Despite Maybelle's instruction, no one else in the room was

seated. Marvin Lee stood in the doorway, his hands on his hips as he looked at and listened to his mother with the rapt attention reminiscent of his boyhood.

Jubal stood in the same spot where he had entered the room. The window fan blowing on his sweat-soaked clothes cooled his body, but it did nothing to assuage the turmoil he was feeling. Jenny stood on the other side of the room, just the hint of a tear in her eye as she took in the situation. They looked at each other, not really listening to Maybelle, their minds focused more on each other, realizing that their current situation was just one part of their predicament.

Nobody said anything as Maybelle, the adjudicator, puffed on her cigarette and pondered what to do next. Finally, she said, "Alright, here's the deal. Marvin Lee, you ain't gonna say nothin' 'bout this 'til in the mornin', at which time you will come and get young Jubal here and take him to the office; then you and the sheriff can figure out how to get him back with his mama. Jenny, me and you gonna have a long talk tonight 'bout a lotta things, and I'll decide in the mornin' what to do with you. Jubal, you gonna call your mama right now from that phone right there in my kitchen and let her know you're alright, and I'll want to talk to her myself just to make her feel better."

Having made her pronouncement, Maybelle put out her cigarette in the ashtray on the table beside her, rose and left the room. Marvin Lee turned to leave and said, "I'll see y'all in the mornin'."

Jenny walked over and took both of Jubal's hands in hers and said, "It'll be alright. You'll see."

"Come on in here, Jubal, and call your mama!" came the agitated voice from the kitchen.

Jenny smiled and squeezed Jubal's hands as he left for the kitchen. It was only a few steps to the kitchen where Maybelle stood by the phone that sat on the kitchen counter. But Jubal felt alone and far away as he left Jenny standing in the living room.

Maybelle picked up the phone, dialed zero, then spoke authoritatively to the operator, "Louise, this is Maybelle Sykes. I got a young man that needs to make a call to… hold on. You tell her," she said as she handed the phone to Jubal.

"Taggart, Virginia, please. TA3-3954," he instructed. The phone only rang a couple of times before Jubal's mother answered, "Hello."

"Mama, this is Jubal. I…" was all he could say before his mother began to cry and talk at the same time.

"Jubal, are you alright?" she wept into the phone.

"Yes, ma'am. I'm fine. We're staying with a nice lady, and I'll probably be coming home tomorrow. I still haven't caught up with Mac yet. I hate for him to leave to fight that war without me. I…"

"Oh, Jubal, Jubal, Jubal! You can't fight a war. Not with Mac or anybody else. You're not old enough. You don't even know what war is. Now come on home and quit this foolishness before you get hurt or something worse. I miss you so and I want you safe with me. I don't know what I'd do if something were to happen to you," she sobbed.

Jubal was about to cry too. It hurt him to hear his mother weeping. He had not thought she would be so upset. "I'll be coming home tomorrow, Mama. You don't have to worry anymore. I'm really alright. Miss Maybelle Sykes is taking good care of me. Here, talk to her. She'll tell you. I love you, Mama."

Maybelle took the phone from Jubal, who left the kitchen to sit out on the steps of the back porch. "Miss Simpson, this here is Maybelle Sykes down in Minot Springs, North Carolina. Your boy is alright. He ain't hurt, he's doing fine and I'm fixin' to cook him a good meal. I done washed his clothes, and I'll make sure he gets a good night's sleep 'fore I send back to you in the mornin'. Now, I know it don't do no good to tell you not to worry 'cause I know you will 'til you set your own eyes on him. I got a boy too so I know how you feel. My boy's a man now 'cording to age, but long as I live he'll always be my boy. Fact is, it's my boy'll be pickin' yours up here in the mornin' to make sure he gets back to you."

"Oh, Miss Sykes, I am so appreciative of all you've done for Jubal. He is my life, and I don't know what I'd do if anything were to happen to him. I don't know how he happened to come to you, but I feel sure God had a hand in it. Thank you so much."

"Well, you are welcome, ma'am. 'Tween me and the Lord,

we'll get him back to you in good shape. Sometimes I wish the Lord'd give me a little warning when he's settin' things up. It'd be a lot less stressful on my end."

After the two ladies had finished their conversation, Maybelle called Jenny to come into the kitchen to help her fix supper. "Come on in here, girl. I don't know how much you know about cookin', but we'll find out. I have found that you can learn a whole lot about somebody when they labor beside you. Ain't no barriers between you. There's a tin pot of butterbeans over yonder on the counter. You shell 'em while I get this corn shucked and boilin'; then we'll see about some rice to go with some pork chops Marvin Lee got at the Piggly Wiggly yesterday.

"When me and Mr. Sykes got married, I weren't much older than you. I had six brothers and four sisters in a little bitty house over toward Ten Mile Creek. He didn't have nothin' to recommend him as a husband. He was skinny as a rail and ugly as a burnt stump, but I won't gonna be picky. I was lookin' to leave home soon as I could, and he was the first one to come along to give me the chance. But he was a good man with a good heart, and he had a job over to Jameson's saw mill.

"It wasn't 'til after we was married and he'd come in the kitchen to help me cook that I figured I had lucked up and got a good'n that I could love. I weren't much older'n you. I didn't know what I was gettin' into but, like I said, I was lucky."

Maybelle continued to shuck the corn, and Jenny shelled the beans in silence. Shortly Maybelle said, "I guess since you ain't gonna tell me 'less I ask you so I just need to come out and ask you 'bout your feelin' toward Jubal. It don't take a smart person to see that y'all care about each other. 'Course, most folks'd say you ain't neither one old enough to know about feelin's and such. Ain't necessarily so. See, there's different kinds of feelin's. There's fear and happiness and sadness and joy and love and hate and all kinds of shades in between. You can have them feelin's when you're young and when you're old; and sometimes though, particularly when you're young, you don't know when you got 'em 'til somebody who has had 'em tells you. Even then it's hard to tell what you got. You just use what they tell you as reference. Well, I'm here to tell you, girl. I've had 'em. All of 'em. What kinda feelin's you think you got?"

Jenny had not said much since she and Jubal had arrived at Maybelle's house, and now she didn't know what to say. She just kept on shelling butterbeans as if they were rosary beads, some source of solace to calm the confusion she felt. When she and Jubal had left Longview, her whole life changed. The fact that she couldn't honestly remember much about Longview and that life contributed to her confusion. Maybelle's rambling philosophy was incomprehensible. She was just a girl in a new world on an uncharted journey with no particular destination. How could she explain what she had never felt before or even thought of before?

She wanted to respond to Maybelle's kindness. She wanted to understand what was happening to her. But the only words that came to mind were the same words she had said to Jubal, "It'll be alright. You'll see."

While Jenny and Maybelle had remained in the kitchen, Jubal had been sitting on the back-porch steps listening to the one-sided conversation. He strained to hear what Jenny would say to Maybelle's question. It was essential to his effort to understand his own feelings. It seemed to be a futile process.

After supper, Jenny and Jubal sat on the back porch in the quiet of the evening as the sun slipped behind the big clouds. They had not said much during the meal as Maybelle continued to carry on about her life with Mr. Sykes. They had both offered to wash the dishes; but Maybelle declined the offer saying, "Y'all just go on out there on the porch and take in the air. Evening air tends to clear things up, you know."

Jubal resumed his spot on the steps, and Jenny claimed a straw-bottomed, ladder-backed chair on the end of the porch. The background clatter of pots and pans being cleaned mixed with the rustle of the leaves in the giant old pecan trees and the rhythmical sound of crickets chirping their overture to the coming night. The distant rumble of thunder provided tympani to nature's nocturnal symphony. The breeze seemed more cooling than the electric fan in the living room. The tiny night wind was soft and calming, even as its force ebbed and flowed across the fields and through the trees. It created a pensive mood that made Jubal want to reach out and touch Jenny, to give some tactile sensation to an intangible, indefinable yearning.

The spell was broken by Maybelle's brusque exit from the kitchen. She backed through the screen door, using her body to open it since she held a freshly-lit cigarette in one hand and a glass of amber liquid in the other. She deposited herself on a short, three-legged wooden stool beside Jenny. The stool was low enough that it caused Maybelle's short legs to bend so that she could place a wrist on each kneecap as she held out her cigarette and drink.

"Y'all got everything figured out?" she asked bluntly with no response. She lifted her glass and said, "This here helps me figure out stuff sometimes. Kinda gentles my mind. 'Course, I can't give y'all none of it."

The trio sat quietly on the porch as the sky pulled in black clouds that began to slowly shed a few large raindrops splattering singularly in the dusty yard before a precluding clap of thunder sent the rain tumbling down. Jubal quickly retreated to the shelter of the porch; but it didn't shield him from the rain being driven by the wind, a wind very unlike the breeze that had lulled him just a few minutes earlier. Repeating bursts of thunder crashed around them and were quickly succeeded by flashes of lightning that seemed nearer with each thrust into the aerial turmoil.

"Come on, young'uns. We need to go ahead on in outta this mess," urged Maybelle. She flipped her cigarette out into the wet melee, tossed the contents of her drink behind it, then reached for the screen door, Jenny and Jubal crowding behind her. Just as she grasped the door handle, a resounding clap of thunder shook the house; and a bright flash of light reflected behind them with a simultaneous explosion that crashed through the air like cannon fire.

"Good god a'mighty!" exclaimed Maybelle as the already soaking-wet trio turned to look behind them. "The damned lightnin's hit my 'bacca barn!" she shouted as she rushed out into the driving rain toward the barn.

Jenny and Jubal stood like statues frozen by the storm as they watched Maybelle run through the rain, the brittle, leaf-heavy pecan limbs falling around her creating an arboreal gauntlet as she raced to save the most valuable property she had: the building that held a portion of the crop she depended on for her livelihood.

By the time Jubal reached the barn, the top of the building was engulfed in flames shooting high into the wind-driven rain that failed to diminish the blaze. The wide shelter that went around all four sides of the barn provided little cover for Maybelle or Jubal as they rushed to the wide, low door of the barn. Maybelle turned the latch, a single piece of wood nailed in the middle to the door facing. It turned easily; and as Maybelle jerked the door open, a wall of flame pushed the door open so quickly that it knocked Maybelle down, taking Jubal with her. They jumped up quickly, retreating into the rain as it poured down impotently on the inferno. The entire barn was on fire, encompassing everything under the shelter. A rack of tobacco sticks that had been stored for the next morning's process of hanging the replacement for the now-ruined crop burned like bundled torches.

As Maybelle stood in the rain watching her world diminish in the conflagration, she suddenly shouted, "Run, boy, run!" as she grasped Jubal's arm and starting running down through the tobacco field, the sticky green leaves of the tall plants slapping at both of them, grasping at them. They had only gone a few feet when they felt the blast of a tremendous explosion so strong that it blew the tobacco plants to the ground and threw pieces of wood and tin roofing over the retreating pair as they too were forced onto the wet ground. "That was the oil tank," said Maybelle as she looked back at the barn, now a pile of rubble throwing off sparks that danced like red demons in the pelting rain. The fragrant smell of burning tobacco blended with the odor of old wood and kerosene as the remnants of the barn glowed and smoldered.

Maybelle and Jubal sat silently in the muddy field. Rain continued to come down on them unabated, the same kind of rain that had fed the tobacco plants, nourished them after the summer drought, the same kind of rain that had cooled the steamy nights as

Maybelle made the trek from her house to check on the curing process in the barn that now lay reduced to ashes. It was the same kind of rain that had lulled her to sleep so many nights as she slept under the barn shelter so she could keep a close watch on the curing tobacco.

"The Lord gives and the Lord takes away," muttered Maybelle.

Jubal looked at the woman beside him and knew, even with his limited exposure to life, that this was a big deal, that it was lifechanging. "Whatcha gonna do, Miss Maybelle?" he asked with concern and sympathy.

"Hell, boy, we just get up and keep on goin'," she answered as she pushed herself up from the muddy field and walked past the barn, through the red raindrops reflecting the flames and toward her house.

Jubal remained there in the muddy tobacco field, steam rising from his body as the cold rain met the intense heat that had enclosed him. He watched Maybelle walk away and he felt very much alone.

Then he remembered Jenny. Where was she? He had left her on the porch when he chased Maybelle to the burning barn. He quickly rose and ran toward the house, rushed past Maybelle, onto the porch and into the house. He searched frantically for her; and when he couldn't find her, he rushed back out of the house, heedless of the rain and the wind. The thunder and lightning slipped away into the night, and Jubal realized that so had Jenny.

He returned to the porch and sat on the chair where Jenny had sat just a short time ago. He unconsciously hoped that he could somehow still feel her there. But she was gone.

Why? he silently asked himself. So many *whys*. Why had she left? Why did he feel alone? They barely knew each other and only for a short time. Why would he have such a feeling of loss? He wanted to cry but he thought, *Men don't cry. I'm almost a man.* But he cried anyway.

Chapter 13

When Miss Jane got the call from Maybelle, she immediately called Chief Gains. Of course, the chief called the Minot Springs sheriff's office, and they said they would meet whoever was coming to pick up Jubal at the station the next morning. That "whoever" turned out to be me and Leon. Chief Gains said he'd appreciate it if we'd go pick up Jubal since he really didn't have any deputies or cars to spare. We went over to the station to get the authorization papers we needed to pick up and transport Jubal back home. Chief Gains made us temporary deputies. I thought it unique, to say the least, that I couldn't vote but I could be an officer of the law. It made me question the legality of my appointment.

I felt a little better about our trip that time since the chief had given us a detailed road map and directions to Minot Springs, NC. It was about a four- hour drive to our destination. As I looked at the map, I realized that it looked like Minot Springs was approximately a hundred miles north of Fayetteville, the city where Fort Bragg was located. Jubal had done well, given the fact that he didn't know exactly where he was going or how to get there.

I figured the road to Minot Springs would be a long one in more ways than just the miles. My previous drive with Leon had not included much conversation. I was glad there was a radio in the hearse so we could listen to some music on the way. I wasn't sure why the radio was in a hearse since whoever was driving, which would be Leon, wouldn't turn it on if there was a body in the back; that would have been disrespectful.

When we were out looking for Jubal on that other trip, Leon didn't turn the radio on until we were headed back to Taggart. By that time of night, you could only get a few powerful stations like the one in Cincinnati or New Orleans or Chicago or some other far-off place. Most of the local stations went off the air at sundown, and during the day you had to change the station about every thirty miles or so.

Mama liked to listen to WWVA in Wheeling, West Virginia. She told me that she and Daddy would listen to a live country music show called "Jamboree" back before the war so she listened to it a lot when he was away. Dad only listened to the local news and sometimes on Saturday afternoon, he'd tune in to a broadcast of the Metropolitan Opera. Mama liked country, Dad liked opera after the war. He said he sometimes listened to country music just to remind him of Mama.

Dad didn't talk much about the war. He had been a reporter for *The Stars and Stripes* and had covered most of the war in Europe. He said he had seen some of the great music halls destroyed by war; and it seemed that listening to the music that had once graced those venues was his way of keeping that art alive, a way of remembering something good about a place that had otherwise held only memories of death and destruction.

As opposed to the previous trip, Leon was in a good mood as we left Taggart. He was wearing a tan suit and a red tie, his black shoes were shined to a high gloss and he was humming along with the song playing on the local station when he said, "Go ahead and find whatever you want to listen to on there. Doesn't matter much to me. I like all kinds of music. I'd just as soon you didn't play any of that rock-and-roll stuff, though. That's not real music."

I guess he felt good about going to get Jubal because he knew that would make Miss Jane happy. Leon was the first man I ever knew who was in love, or at least in what I understood to be love at the time. How he felt was evidently pretty much determined by how Miss Jane felt. I guess that's how love works.

So we listened for a little while until the static got so bad we couldn't pick up anything. "Sometimes hard to get a signal going up and down these mountains," he declared. "I like all kinds of music, you know. Play a little myself. Little piano. Not enough to entertain anybody but myself."

"You ever play for Miss Jane?" I asked.

"Yeah, every once in a while I'll play something when I'm over to her house. She always tells me how much she likes whatever I play," he said with a smile. Again, I thought, *that's how love works.*

145

I asked Leon how he got into the funeral business. If I had known how that question was going to affect him, I wouldn't have asked. His smile faded, and he didn't answer me right away. "When the war came, I was just a little older than you are now. I was a lot like you and Jubal: grew up in Taggart, went to high school there, played in the band, school plays, just like y'all, never been more than twenty miles from home. I was going to UVA, going to major in engineering. I'd only been there a few months when war was declared. I wanted to join the Army and see the world, fight for my country, be a hero in some great battle, come back home famous! So I joined up.

"When I got ready to leave basic training, the Army decided I would best serve my country in the special units. They had learned I played the trumpet in the high school band. I thought that meant I'd be playing for the USO shows or something. But it didn't. I was assigned to the Army Military District of Washington, which was in charge of military funerals. They shared my talents with other military units all over the country. Trumpet players must have been hard to come by. I was supposed to only be there a short while; but instead I played taps for military funerals for the next four years, so when I got out, that's all I had to offer as a job reference.

"So I came home, went to work for the Bates Funeral home in Taggart and that's where I've been ever since. When Mr. Bates died, I bought the business. No glory, no hero. But I do know how to conduct a funeral better than just about anybody."

I probably should have told him that he was a hero. I'm pretty sure all those families who heard him play taps at the funerals of their loved ones thought he was. Sometimes I believe real heroes come in disguise.

As we headed south, the big white clouds began to get darker. Pretty soon a few big raindrops splattered the windshield. Leon turned on the windshield wipers, but they only smeared the dirt and bugs on the glass so he turned them off until the glass was wet enough for the wipers to be effective. In just a few seconds, the rain became a torrent so strong that Leon had to slow the car. "This ain't good, Raymond," he said as he used his hand to wipe the mist off the inside of the windshield. "I can't hardly see where I'm going. I can't even see how to get off the road."

As thunder sounded around us, Leon slowed the car to just a crawl and peered over the steering wheel as if being closer to the windshield would improve his vision. I could tell we were going downhill, but I couldn't see where we were going any more than Leon could. The wind had picked up enough that I could feel it blowing against the car

Suddenly I felt the car lurch forward and jolt to a halt. I looked out the side window and saw that the front wheel was in a ditch. We had been going so slowly that it looked like we had just set down in the ditch, no sliding, no banging into anything—we just ran off the road.

Leon turned off the motor and just looked ahead as the rain continued to pour over us. "Well, I always sleep better when I hear rain on the roof," he said calmly as he leaned his head on the back of the seat and closed his eyes. I followed his action, but I couldn't go to sleep. I kept thinking that some other vehicle, the driver as sightless as we were, might come up and hit our car from behind. I wondered if I would be safer out in the rain further from the car. I'd rather be hit by the pelting rain than a car so I got out of the car and stepped toward the ditch. It was a small, shallow ditch so I just stepped across it and headed toward what appeared to be the woods on the other side.

When I got to the edge of the woods, the rain wasn't plunging down on me; and I looked back at the hearse and saw that it was, just as I figured, resting with the two front wheels in the shallow ditch and the back end of the vehicle still on the edge of the road, which was just beginning a steep, curvy incline. It occurred to me that now would be a good time for Leon to turn on the emergency light on top of the hearse. I couldn't get any wetter so I started back toward the hearse to wake Leon up and get him to put the emergency signal up.

I had only gone a few steps before I heard the crash. It wasn't really a crash as much as just a loud bump, no squealing of tires even. Obviously, the other car wasn't going very fast because the collision was so small that the hearse had not even moved. As I got closer to the hearse, I still couldn't see the car that had hit the hearse since it was on the other side from me. As I walked around the back end of the hearse, it was apparent why I couldn't see the car. It wasn't a car. It was a bicycle: a two-seater, a bicycle built for two. It was lying on the pavement beside two people, a man and a woman, both of whom began to stand up as I approached.

"Are y'all hurt?" I asked.

"Naw, I think we're alright, just scratched up a little bit maybe," responded the man. He was an older man, maybe sixty years old, with long grey hair pulled back into a pony tail. He wore khaki pants and a thin denim shirt like sailors wear and no shoes. "Just got going downhill and couldn't stop or make the turn," he continued as he reached down for the handlebars of the bicycle.

"I tried to stop it, but all I did was pedal backwards. That thing's not connected right," spoke the woman as she bent down to pick her glasses off the pavement. She was dressed in a pair of men's jeans and a flannel shirt… and no shoes. Her hair was also grey and hung in soaking wet strands around her heavily-wrinkled face. "Looks like you were pedaling backward too," she said as she gestured toward the hearse. She walked over to the driver's side door and rubbed the surface of the car. "Don't believe we did it too much damage. Come on, J.W., let's get the man back on the road."

Even with all the commotion, Leon had not made his presence known. "My friend Leon is actually the driver," I said as I reached

149

to open the door. Leon wasn't there. I bent down and looked in the back of the hearse to see if he might have crawled back there to take his nap. He wasn't there. I stood back up and anxiously looked around for Leon. He wasn't there. I began to panic. I had only been gone from the hearse just a minute before it was rammed by the bicycle. How could he have just vanished that quickly?

"Leon!" I shouted to the wet hillside. "Come on now. We need to get outta this rain and get on down the road." Nothing. No reply.

"Leon!" I shouted as I ran back up the road in the direction we had just come from. "Leon!"

I stood there in the middle of the road waiting for a response that never came. I was at once afraid for what had happened to Leon and what had happened to me. We had been a pair united in a quest to find Jubal. Now my friend had mysteriously disappeared, and I didn't know what to do. "Leon, where are you?" I cried into the rain.

"Come on, boy. Let's get your vehicle back on the road and maybe we can find your friend," came the voice of the man behind me. I dazedly turned and walked back toward the hearse. "Can you drive?" he asked.

"No," I replied. "I haven't got a license."

"You don't have to have a license to be able to drive; you just need to know how," the woman said.

"Come on. Get in the car and take it out of gear," instructed the man as he and the woman went to the front of the car. I got in the car and tried to move the gear shift on the steering column, but it wouldn't budge. "Push in the clutch and shift!" shouted the man, but I didn't know what the clutch was. The man evidently sensed my dilemma and said, "It's the pedal on the left!" I pushed in the clutch and pulled the gear shift down and almost immediately I felt the front of the car come up just a little as the two bicyclists pushed on the car.

"Alright, push, Ella," said the man; I felt the car ease backward onto the road, then continue to roll back down the incline. "Put on the brake!" shouted the man. I had never driven before, but I figured if the clutch were on the left, the brake must be on the right so I jammed my foot onto the brake and stopped the hearse in the middle of the road and just sat there with my arms looped around the steering wheel and my head resting on the top of my hands. *There's bound to be a better way to learn to drive*, I thought.

Ella came over to the hearse and opened the door. "Okay, son, we'll take it from here. Slip over," she said.

As I moved over to the middle of the seat, the man put the bicycle in the back of the hearse, then came around and sat on the right side of the seat.

Surprised that the woman was driving since the man had been giving me instructions, I asked him, "You can't drive?"

"Nope. Used to but I gave up all modern conveyances when I shook off the restricting coil of today's civilization," he answered.

151

"Names J.W., by the way," he added as he reached to shake my hand. "Yours?" he asked.

"Raymond Lovejoy, Jr.," I answered. "I always add the 'Jr.' so people don't get me confused with my father."

"Good idea," said J.W. with a smile, then sighed, "Okay. We got to decide where we're going from here. What is your destination, Raymond Lovejoy, Jr.?"

"Leon and I were going to pick up my friend, Jubal, in a town called… I forgot the name, but it's somewhere in North Carolina. I don't know where it is, but Leon did… does." The return of the realization of Leon's disappearance struck me hard and quick. "We need to find Leon before we go anywhere!" I shouted as I pushed against J.W. to get out of the hearse.

"And where you going to look for him?" asked J.W. as he held my flailing arms.

"I don't know," I said weakly as I realized the futility of my situation.

"I tell you what, Raymond Lovejoy, Jr., I believe Leon is alright and so are you. Nothing happens by accident. Everything in life has a beginning and an end, and all that happens in the middle just gets us from start to finish. We just need to accept things as they are and make the most of every minute. That's the way it is with me and Ella. We don't have a destination; we just live for the moment and in the moment. There are no challenges, just a continuous,

152

spontaneous reaction to events. Now, since Ella and I have no destination, we'll adopt yours. That means we're going on down this road in the direction you and Leon were headed and see what happens."

There was something comforting in J.W.'s simplistic logic that calmed my fears somewhat. I figured I didn't have any answers so I might as well accept his.

So Ella started the car and shifted into a series of gears as we headed back down the road in the direction from which Ella and J.W. had come.

The rain had slowed to a steady drizzle, cooling the air some; but the humidity still hung in the wetness, making the three of us sitting close together in the seat uncomfortable. Ella and J.W. opened the little window vents on their respective sides of the car, letting in a little cool air along with some water. The smell of our damp clothes didn't help with the comfort level.

We rode in silence for a while with nothing but the rain-shrouded, wooded hillsides for scenery. I had a lot of questions about my rescuers but didn't want to be rude by asking. Mama had told me to never ask strangers personal questions, and I always wanted to do what Mama said. However, I figured those two were not strangers now that we were sharing an uncertain destination and would be together for probably a long time. Besides, I just knew there had to be an interesting story there; and, being the son of a newspaper man, I knew you should always pursue a good story.

"So, where ya'll from?" I asked just to get the conversation started.

"Nowhere and everywhere," answered Ella. "Our origin is insignificant. We just met up and decided we were two unique individuals with matched souls. So we have chosen to share our lives."

"You been married long?"

"We aren't married at all. That's one of those conventions of our culture that we have chosen to ignore. Our commitment is to each other, not to any government or religion or even the dictums of society," asserted J.W.

I didn't know where to go from there. I was apparently riding down the road with people unlike any I knew in Taggart, Virginia. I had heard some of the guys in the press room at the newspaper talk about a former employee who they said was "shacked up" with a woman from over in Newtown. They said my father had fired him because he couldn't have that kind of immorality associated with the paper. Said they should have gotten married to save the man's job. I never asked my father about it. That just wasn't a subject I felt like talking to him about, especially when I didn't know exactly what all was involved in "shacking up."

J.W. sensed my uneasiness and said, "It's alright, son. We accepted the judgment of people a long time ago. When I came back from the war, I had seen enough of what the world thought was proper, some of it in the name of war and some just human depravity hiding behind politics. I determined that the 'proper life' was just a sham, and I was going to lead a life that was right as I saw it. I taught college for about a year and saw that the kids coming along had different goals based on their own experiences that were a lot different from mine, and the college administration was more focused on expanding the campus than expanding the minds of the students. So I left to create my own world that's right in my mind."

"I'll tell you my story later after the shock of J.W.'s wears off," said Ella. She was a very observant woman.

Miles went by with no further conversation. I was left to my own thoughts, not so much about my companions, but more about what had happened to Leon and our effort to retrieve Jubal. I told J.W. I needed to call my dad and let the folks back in Taggart know where we were. He said we'd stop at the next phone booth; but there were no phone booths to be seen, just miles and miles of woods and hills and rain.

Chapter 14

Maybelle fixed a good supper of fried pork chops, stewed tomatoes and rice and fried okra after she got Jubal's cleaned clothes out for him and some dry clothes for herself. Jubal hadn't said anything during the meal although Maybelle tried to get him to talk.

"She'll probably come on back when she gets things sorted out in her mind," she said, trying to console Jubal. "Kinda like you, you know. Y'all been through a lot in a right short amount of time. She'll probably be back here before mornin'."

The good food and Maybelle's effort to make him feel better didn't have much effect on Jubal. He knew Jenny wasn't coming back and somebody from Taggart would be there to take him back next morning. He knew he would never see Jenny again. His black mood was so dark he didn't even think about his original goal of joining Mac. His whole world had changed. All the images of the people he had gotten to know in the past few days flashed through his mind: Billy and the Rev. Branson, Clement and the boys in the band, Prince Albert Watson and Maybelle and Jenny... mostly Jenny. Seemed like it was many years ago when he decided to chase after Mac. *What a stupid thing that was,* he thought. Now they were all gone, and he was going back to Taggart. It just wouldn't be the same.

Maybelle had tried to console him with food and optimism, but she could tell it wasn't having the desired effect so she decided to try another tack. "Life's a bitch, ain't it?" she said after getting no response to her more sympathetic approach. "The odds just stacked against you. No matter how bright things look, something'll come along and 'fore you know it, the world's just one black hole. Let's go sit on the porch. I'll wash the dishes later."

Reluctantly Jubal followed Maybelle out to the porch, the screen door slamming behind him, a fatalistic sound of finality that only enhanced Jubal's sense that he couldn't go back to things as they had been. He purposely didn't sit in the chair where Jenny had sat but chose to sit on the steps. Maybelle sat in the rocking chair behind him and lit a cigarette.

"So what you goin' to do, boy? Sit around and feel sorry for yourself? Say, 'Poor pitiful me. I think I'll just go out and eat worms'?"

Jubal still didn't say anything. The smell of burning wood and tobacco still drifted in the evening air, and from the porch they could see the embers of the tobacco barn glowing in the darkness. Occasionally an ember would pop as it settled, sending sparks into the sky.

Maybelle took a puff of her cigarette, blew the smoke into the air and said, "Me and you are kinda like that barn there, Jubal. We been dealt a heavy blow. Ain't much left. Farming 'bacca is all I do.

That's my life. I could be like you and say everything's gone and I might as well just give up. But, you know, that ain't me. That barn ain't me. Giving up ain't who I am. Starting tomorrow I'm goin' to call on my neighbors to help me get the rest of my crop in.

Somebody'll have a extra barn. Then I'm goin' to build another barn and plant another crop, and I'm goin' to keep on livin' until the good Lord brings me to a halt.

"Now in your case, you don't even know what you lost. Ain't no doubt in my mind that Jenny means a lot to you; and I think you're kinda confused about your feelin's and all, but the biggest thing worryin' you is why'd she run off and leave you. Well, I'll tell ya. I might be a lot older than her, but I'm a woman just like she is; and she don't no more know her mind than you do yours. That's the way it's been 'tween male and female since Adam and Eve and ain't likely to change. She run off 'cause she didn't know her mind and she couldn't make it up 'fore the folks get here in the mornin'. You just can't put a deadline on something as important as love. There, I said it. Love. And you don't even know what that is. Some folks say that young love ain't real and ain't real important in the long run. That ain't so. It's real to you and it's real to Jenny even if neither one of you can define it. You just got to give yourself some more time, boy. Jenny had to have more time so she took it by runnin' off. Now, that's about all the advice I can give you. I ain't much qualified to tell other people how to make decisions. I made some bad ones, but I learned from 'em."

Jubal listened to Maybelle's analysis of his problem without comment. But he did consider it and agreed with it. He needed time and he needed to do something. Just like Maybelle would rebuild her barn, he would rebuild his relationship with Jenny. But first he had to find her.

Chapter 15

Ella had not said much as we drove through the rain toward our unknown destination. But as the sky began to clear enough to see where we were going, darkness began to creep into the woods.

"Need to find something to eat and someplace to sleep," she said matter-of-factly as if that were just the next step in our journey and not the major consideration that it was.

"We're not too far from Longview. That's our best bet," said J.W.

"I don't know. You know what that situation is. They may not let us come back," Ella replied.

"Oh, I think they will. Jubal's with us," asserted J.W.

I didn't understand why my presence would allow people I didn't know to get into a place I had never been. Then again, everything about this couple was strange. My world had been Taggart, Virginia. I had been born there in the middle of The Great Depression, never traveled further than Martinsville. The only people I knew were people just like me. There was nobody like J.W. and Ella. If this strange couple needed me to get into wherever they were going, then that place had to be as strange as they were.

So we drove on through the darkness toward the place called

Longview. I was tired and the monotony of the drive eased me to sleep despite my anxiety about where we were going. I was awakened by the sound of weeds and brush scraping the underside and sides of the hearse. Night had fully descended, but Ella had not turned on the headlights of the hearse; and darker shadows whipped by us as we proceeded down what appeared to be a narrow dirt road. Then I saw the periphery of light above the treetops. In just a few minutes, that light expanded to show a whole town lined out before us. It was a perfect little town that looked as if somebody had modeled it after a painting on a calendar. But there were no people.

"Yep, I told you they wouldn't let us back in," said Ella as we surveyed the beautiful, quiet, empty town.

"Well, we haven't been totally rejected; we just haven't been admitted yet," said J.W. as he looked around the town for some evidence of life. "Pull over there to Miss Arlene's store. She's always open, and she's too kind to turn us away."

Ella parked the hearse in front of a small wooden building with a sign above a narrow porch that said "Arlene's Grocery." The three of us entered the store through a narrow double door into a brightly-lit room filled with every imaginable item from clothes to food of all kinds. There was no one in the room, but there was a small table set up just inside the door. On the table was a sheet of notebook paper on which was written, "YOU MAY EAT WHATEVER FOOD YOU NEED. DON'T BE GREEDY. YOU MAY SLEEP IN

THE BARN, BUT BE GONE BY TOMORROW NIGHT. TELL JUBAL NOT TO LEAVE UNTIL I TALK TO HIM. ARLENE."

"She knew we were coming," said Ella.

"Of course, she did," said J.W. "This is Longview."

"How did she know about me?" I asked in amazement.

"This is Longview," repeated J.W.

So we gathered some bread and milk and some sandwich materials from the little meat market and went back out the front door, then walked around to the back of the building where we saw a barn with a small paddock beside it. J.W. led the way after he slid the wide door open and entered the building. Just inside the door was a kerosene lantern. Beside the lantern hung a box of large matches tied with a string to the nail on which the lantern was attached. After J.W. lit the lantern, he walked around the area shining the soft light into each corner of the one-room building. It was a small barn that had not been used in a long time but was as clean as much as barns can be clean. On one wall was a spigot with a green water hose attached. The building was not intended for human habitation, but as Ella said, "Any port in a storm."

There were about thirty bales of hay stacked on one side. They had apparently just been cut since the smell was pleasantly fresh and there was no dust. J.W. took one of the bales and tore it apart, scattering it in one corner. As he tore up and spread other bales, he instructed me to do the same on the opposite side of the barn.

"Not too bad," he said. "We've got food and shelter for the night, neither of which cost us anything."

While we had been literally making our beds for the night, Ella had prepared our supper. We ate the sandwiches and shared the milk by passing the glass jar around. When we finished, J.W. said, "Well, Raymond, Ella will now tell you her story. It is indeed a bedtime story." For a man who professed to have no agenda, J.W. seemed to have the evening scheduled pretty well.

"I don't know if I can just tell my story on cue, J.W.," said Ella. "My life does not lend itself to narrative recitation, and I don't know if Raymond's young life has enough experience to provide a reference that would illustrate or illuminate the words I would have to use. I'm not a storyteller like you are; and although my past has involved relationships with many people, I am essentially a private person. I might need to know more about Raymond before I can share what I have shared with only a few people with whom I have felt comfortable. You know that; look how long it took me to confide in you."

Ella's reluctance to tell me about her life only made me more curious although I had not voiced my curiosity about either of them. Evidently J.W. was more anxious to share their story than Ella was.

"I'm sorry, dear, I didn't mean to embarrass you or put any pressure on you. I just thought… well, I've got a feeling that Raymond is a lot like us in many ways; but he's just beginning to have those experiences you mentioned. I thought we might help him be more prepared and, at the same time, help him appreciate those experiences when they do come along."

"Well, maybe you're right," acknowledged Ella. "But I will tell you this, Raymond. Sometimes it's facing new experiences without knowing what to expect that makes them more exciting and worthwhile. When we get better acquainted, I'll probably help you some, tell you things that'll make you laugh and some that'll curl your hair and some that's downright unbelievable! But right now all of us need to get a good night's sleep. Raymond, you sleep over there where you spread that hay; and J.W. and I will sleep over here. You need to get rid of those wet clothes too before you catch your death of cold. Just take 'em off and hang 'em over that rafter over there. Don't worry, no need to be embarrassed. Believe me, I've seen enough naked bodies that yours won't even be noted."

Although Ella was not at all like my mother, she spoke with a maternal authority that made me do as she said without questioning. The corner of the barn that was to be my bedroom for the night was far enough away from the lantern light that I felt a certain amount of privacy as I shed my wet clothes and hung them across the rafter over my head. I pushed enough hay together to make a semblance of a bed, laid down on it and pulled some more hay over me. Apart from being a little scratchy, it was fairly comfortable; and the smell of new-mown hay combined with weariness made sleep descend on me whether I wanted it to or not. In the fog of my mind just before sleep overcame me, I saw Ella drape her clothes over a rafter on the other side of the barn. I had never seen a woman without clothes on.

I believe that seeing Ella's mature body in the glow of the lantern light was one of those occasions that she was talking about when she said some experiences are more exciting when they are unexpected. I slept fitfully.

Chapter 16

Jubal didn't go to sleep that night. He lay in the bed thinking of how he was going to find Jenny. He had no real idea of where she might have run off to. They had known each other such a short time that she had not shared with him any history of her life that might give him a clue as to where she might go. His first thought was she would go back home. But where was home? All he could remember was what she had said that night they escaped from Longview:

"Longview is a place that just is… and now I am here."

He determined that his only course of action was to find Longview. If Jenny wasn't there, maybe someone in the town would know where she was.

The sun was barely above the treetops as Jubal put on his clothes and stepped as lightly as he could down the short hallway into the living room on his way out the front door of Maybelle's house.

"You might want a bite of breakfast 'fore you go traipsin' off," came Maybelle's voice behind him.

Startled by the voice in the silence of the morning, Jubal turned to see Maybelle standing in the hallway. She stood barefoot in a light-green flannel nightgown, and her grey hair was tousled from an uneasy sleep. She was not a morning vision of inspiration.

"Come on. I knew you were going to go after her. You might oughta get some food in you 'cause it could be a while 'fore you get another chance to eat," she continued as she turned and walked back toward the kitchen. Jubal followed as instructed.

As Maybelle prepared a substantial breakfast of grits, fried eggs, bacon and a large glass of milk, she asked Jubal the obvious question, "Where you goin'?"

"To Longview," he answered.

"And where is Longview?"

"I don't know exactly. It's where we came from. Where Jenny came from, actually."

"So you just goin' to go back the way you came, huh?"

"Yes, ma'am. It's the only place I know to look."

"Well, I gotta tell ya, it ain't the smartest thing for you to do. First of all, you got some folks from Taggart goin' to be here in a little while, and they gonna want to know how come I let you go; and it don't matter what I tell 'em… far as they're concerned, I done wrong. It won't help none that my son is the deputy sheriff, and I have let you escape from his custody. Second, if you don't know where you goin', how you gonna know when you get there?"

"I'll know it when I see it."

"And you'll see it because of your great sense of direction that got you here, right?"

Jubal had almost finished eating his breakfast when he placed his fork on the table, took a last swallow of milk and stood up.

"Listen, Miss Maybelle, I really appreciate all you've done for me; but I just gotta go find Jenny. Tell whoever comes from Taggart that when I find her, I'll be coming home. That's about the only thing I know to do." Then he stood up and walked down the hall toward the front door. Just as he opened the door, he suddenly turned around and walked quickly back into the kitchen, wrapped his arms around Maybelle's small body and said, "Thank you," then ran from the house into the cool morning air.

Jubal ran down the gravel driveway back toward the highway, but he stopped abruptly when he got to the mailbox. "Which way did we come in?" he asked himself. He had been in the back of Marvin Lee's patrol car and was not really paying a lot of attention to where they were going when they had arrived the previous day. There were large cornfields on both sides of the road in both directions. He closed his eyes and tried to remember how they had arrived. He remembered that the mailbox had been on his side of the car when they turned in; and that meant that since he was seated directly behind Marvin Lee, they been coming from the left. So he began to walk slowly in that direction.

The dew was still heavy on the weeds that grew along the roadside causing his shoes to get wet so he walked onto the pavement. He could still smell, even at a distance, the burnt tobacco barn and the clinging odor of the tobacco that had been consumed in the blaze. He realized that a lot had happened in such a short time. It occurred to him that in the midst of all the drama of the fire and Jenny running away, he had not even thought about Mac. His original mission, so urgent and necessary before, now seemed almost insignificant. It wasn't that he didn't want to be with his brother because he really did. But now, looking back, he questioned his reasoning for wanting to join him in the military. That thing about his ancestors fighting together in The Civil War wasn't really a rational association. He knew that war had taken place in a different time, a time when everything was different. War was different. Families were different. The military was different. His idea to join Mac wasn't logical. So why did he come up with such a crazy idea? Could it have been that he didn't want his world to change? If Mac went into the Army, he, Jubal, would be the man of the house, a boy taking up a man's responsibility.

Yeah, there was Leon but he couldn't ever be real family. Even if he and his mother got married, Jubal would still feel responsible for her. No matter who she married, she was still his mother. Maybe he was just running away. Like Jenny.

His thoughts were interrupted by the distant sound of a siren behind him. Marvin Lee had probably gone to the house to pick him up, and Maybelle had told him what happened. As the sound of the siren drew closer, Jubal decided he had to get out of sight so he jumped the ditch that ran alongside the road and ducked into the thick, tall field of corn.

The ground in the field was soft and almost mud but not wet enough to slow him down as he ran between the rows. In just a short time, he heard the siren go past him on the highway so he stopped running and just walked, brushing the green leaves of corn away as he went.

The sun had climbed well into the sky and dried the corn leaves making them almost stiff, stiff enough to scratch at his face and hands as he pushed through the field. He had to tilt his head down to keep from having the corn leaves slap his face. That's how he happened to the see the hoof prints cross his path. He immediately thought of the horse he and Jenny had been riding, the one that had run away when Marvin Lee's siren had startled him. He didn't know much about horses; but he had heard that if a horse is turned loose, it would almost always head back toward its home. Jenny's horse had not exactly been turned loose but was loose nonetheless. Jubal surmised that if he followed the horse's tracks, they would lead him back to Longview.

The tracks cut across several rows, then went between the rows for a while before turning across the rows again. Jubal followed this zigzag trail through the tall corn, never knowing in what direction he was going. The horse had knocked over some stalks of corn as he meandered through the field, and that made it a little easier to follow him; but Jubal wondered how long he would be able to follow the prints once they left the cornfield.

He didn't know how long he had been following the horse, but he was glad Maybelle had fixed him a good breakfast. The sun was now mid-sky, and the heat accumulated and settled to simmer in the cornfield. His clothes were wet with sweat; he was thirsty and trudging through the soft field had made his legs ache. So when he saw that the tracks were leading into some woods adjacent to the field, he was thankful for a little shade and hopeful of finding at least some source of water.

Just as he feared, the horse's hoof prints became harder to follow in the woods. Sometimes he would have to go back and forth across an area until he found the track. Still no water and although the sun was not shining in the shade of the trees, the heat continued unabated. Still he kept walking even as the hoof prints became fainter, until he could no longer find any.

He walked all day, never stopping, afraid that if he did, he would lose the tracks; and when he did finally have to stop, he didn't know where he was or even if he were any closer to finding Jenny. In the midst of the woods, he sat down and leaned his back against the base of an old oak tree. Not only was he thirsty, hungry, tired and despairing of ever finding Jenny, he was also alone. In his whole life, he had never been so alone. Sometimes he had been by himself, but he had never felt alone. This time was different. He couldn't talk to anybody about the situation he found himself in. Mac was gone to some foreign country. There was no telephone he could use to call his mother. No school buddies, no preacher, no teacher. So he talked to God. "God, this is not what I had in mind when I left Taggart. In fact, I wasn't really thinkin' at all, I guess. Sometimes I'm just not very smart and I do stupid stuff, but I've always had somebody to bail me out of every fix I've got myself into. This time it's up to me and you to work this out. Actually I guess it's just you since I got nothin' to add to the process. So let me know what I'm supposed to do. Thank you kindly. Amen."

A cooling breeze had begun to blow through the woods even as Jubal prayed. It didn't quench his thirst or squelch his hunger, but it did cool him off a little. He sat there waiting, waiting for God to speak to him, maybe hear some voice from the sky. But he didn't hear anything, just the soft sound of the breeze through the tall pine trees. Then he thought he heard someone speaking. It may have just been a whisper of the wind, or it may have been God speaking; but it sounded a lot like the voice of Maybelle Sykes, "We just get up and keep on going." After a while, when he figured that God had done all he was going to do for that day, he got up and starting walking. The short rest had seemed to revive him a little bit, and he was a little more optimistic and determined.

He shortly emerged onto a little path in the woods, a narrow game trail. He decided to follow it mainly because he had no other option and also because it was mostly free from the natural impediments of brush and fallen limbs that he had walked over and around since entering the woods. It was a clear night with a full moon that illuminated his path. He wasn't worried about losing his way. Somehow he felt rejuvenated. He knew he was going to find Jenny.

Chapter 17

When I got into Longview that night with Ella and J.W., I sensed that the town was a little strange. Whatever doubts I had about that not being the case were erased the next morning. When we emerged from the barn where we had spent the night, the town was empty and silent. It seemed even more ghostly than it had appeared at night, since there was no light to focus my eyes on the buildings and dirt streets. It was just a wide expanse of inanimate objects. There was no movement, not even a breeze to ruffle the leaves on the oak trees that lined the street that bisected the town. It was so silent I could almost hear my heart beat. But it wasn't a ghost town, at least, not like the ghost towns we saw in the old movies: all grey, weather-beaten, crumbling buildings and tumbleweed rolling down the street. The buildings in Longview were clean, newly-painted with neat signs designating a barber shop, a tea room, a service station, a clothing store, even a millinery. Although the street wasn't paved, there were no weeds either... and no power poles for electricity or telephones, although the town had been lighted that night.

The three of us stood in front of Miss Arlene's store and looked past the hearse parked there and surveyed the scene. "Looks like we missed the Welcome Wagon," allowed J.W.

"Now, you aren't really surprised, are you, J.W.?" asked Ella.

"You know the rules."

"What rules?" I asked. My curiosity was leaping in my brain, looking for something to latch onto.

"We used to live here. Great place to live. Everything anybody really needs. Peaceful. Quiet. Friendly. But the rule is, if you leave, you can never come back. So it's like we aren't here. They say we are shunned. Long as nobody speaks to us, we don't exist. But you know something, Ella, there was another rule. Anybody who comes here for the first time has to be welcomed. This is Raymond's first time. Wonder how they're going to resolve that little contradiction."

"It's not really a contradiction, J.W.," said Miss Arlene as she stepped down off the porch of her store.

I don't know how long she had been standing there, but she startled me as she spoke; and I almost fell as I spun around to see who was speaking.

"You are welcome, Raymond. The contradiction J.W.'s talking about isn't really a contradiction at all. We don't reject anyone who leaves here. When they leave, they reject us and we accept their decision. I'm Miss Arlene. You come on in and I'll fix you some breakfast," she said with a smile that reminded me of my Grandmother Lovejoy.

What kind of place is this? I thought. *Who are these people?*

What the hell is going on?

I was hungry. The little food we had eaten the previous night had done very little to meet the needs of a growing boy who was used to eating a lot and often. But something told me it just wouldn't be right for me to accept Miss Arlene's hospitality if she excluded my friends, the people who had rescued me. "I appreciate your invitation, Miss Arlene, but I just can't accept it and leave my friends out here in the street. Thank you anyway," I said as I turned to go up the deserted street.

"Loyalty is a virtue to be rewarded, Raymond. If you feel that you must include your friends, miscreants that they are, I must expand my invitation and invite you all to come in." With that, she turned and went into her store.

There was a small round table on one side of the store next to the meat counter. Miss Arlene motioned us to be seated as she exited the room and returned almost immediately with a breakfast of

French toast, scrambled eggs and bacon. "Here's a little syrup to go with your toast. Ella, I assume you want your usual coffee with cream; and yours is black, J.W., if I remember correctly," said Miss Arlene as if none of the conversation we had had in the street had ever occurred. She seemed genuinely glad to have found a loophole in the rules. "Milk and orange juice for you, Raymond," she said as she placed both items before me.

While we ate, Miss Arlene sat at the table with us and brought

Ella and J.W. up-to-date on what had been going on in Longview.

"You know we don't get much excitement here, but just a few days ago we had a group of traveling minstrels who came into town and provided a great evening of entertainment. We were sorry to see them leave, and I truly believe they would have stayed; but they said they had several engagements scheduled in the big cities so they left. I think they may have left rather hurriedly since they left one of their members behind. But I understand that he has found his own way. Frankly I was disappointed to learn that one of our young ladies who has been a part of Longview almost her whole life chose to expedite the young man's exit and in so doing has, in keeping with the rules, rejected us."

It seemed this town was full of surprises. Apparently, the old observation that appearances are deceiving certainly applied to Longview. Again, my curiosity overcame me and I had to ask,

"How do you know my name and that I was coming?"

"Oh, Mr. Watson came by yesterday and told me to expect you," Miss Arlene answered as if such knowledge of what was going to happen was commonly known.

"And who is Mr. Watson?" I asked.

"He is a man of great mystery," inserted J.W. "Everybody knows him, but nobody seems to know who he is. He comes and goes at irregular intervals. He seems to sense every need in the town; and, before you know it, that need has been met without anyone even voicing a request."

Ella reached over and took Miss Arlene's hand and said, "You may know, Miss Arlene, that the main reason we left Longview had nothing to do with the wonderful people here. It was just that we had no purpose here. We had nothing to offer, and the town had no need for us. We were useless. Mr. Watson took care of everything. We were teachers with no students, servants with no masters. Why have a nurse when no one ever gets sick? Why would anybody want to learn anything if all they had to do to provide for themselves and each other was to rely on Mr. Watson? Why grow vegetables is they can come to your store and get them for free? Why buy a car if you're not going anywhere since everything you could possibly want is here in Longview? That's why the people who want more than what is provided in Longview have to leave to find it. If they want to expand their minds—their lives—they have to go elsewhere, which is what we did."

Miss Arlene put her other hand on top of Ella's and said, "For some of us, Ella, Longview is enough."

"Well, it's not enough for me," I said. "I've got to get on down the road. I'm supposed to be picking up my friend and taking him back home, and the other friend who was driving us has just disappeared so I need to find him too."

"He's right, Miss Arlene," said J.W. "But first we need to get some gasoline. You think you could persuade Virgil to give us some gas so we can help Raymond on his journey? Since we're not staying, I think it would be within the rules for him to help us, to extend the hospitality of Longview, you might say."

"Oh, I don't think that will be a problem. I'll just go ahead and call over to the station and tell him the situation, and I'm sure he'll be glad to help," offered Miss Arlene as she got up from the table and walked over to the phone on the counter. We couldn't hear the conversation; but when Miss Arlene returned to the table, she said, "Virgil said for y'all to come on over and he'll fix you up."

The three of us left the little store and proceeded to get the hearse over to the service station. "You drive," instructed Ella as she gave the keys to J.W.

It wasn't very far so Ella and I decided to walk. As I looked down the street, I could see folks moving around in and out of the buildings, some just standing and talking to each other just like any other town. It seemed that Miss Arlene had somehow activated a temporary suspension of the rules. In the light of day now, Longview seemed perfect.

The scene and the breakfast conversation urged me to ask the obvious question, "Is this heaven, Ella?"

"Nope, not even close," she answered.

"Is it the other place then?"

"Nope, not that either."

"Well, what is it then? I've never seen a place like this. It's so strange it's almost scary, but at the same time it seems like a wonderful place to live."

"Longview is a complicated place, Raymond. When J.W. and I stumbled on this place, we thought it was the perfect place for us; but we soon found out it wasn't. I was a nurse in the war, and I thought I could provide health service to the people here. But they never got sick or hurt. No babies were ever born here, and no one ever died here. J.W. was a teacher, but there was no school. There's a church down there at the end of the street, but there's no preacher. The sign in front of the church says 'I am the Alpha and Omega,' but it's not talking about the church; it's describing Longview. It's the beginning and the end, but there's no middle. It just exists in the moment. And for the people who choose to live here, that's fine with them. They don't worry about what happened in the past, and they aren't concerned with the future. They are perfectly satisfied with the present. In other words, Longview just is."

As we approached the service station, the attendant had just finished putting gasoline in the hearse and was cleaning the windshield. "Good morning, Ella," he said. "Good to see you. Too bad you gotta leave us again." Miss Arlene had evidently extended the waiver of the rules to everybody else in town.

"Nice to see you too, Virgil," replied Ella.

"And nice to see you too, young man," he said as he continued to clean all the windows of the hearse. "You're kinda like this hearse, don't see either one very often—boys or hearses. Kinda interesting that we had both show up right here lately. Had a boy come by just the other day, traveling with a bluegrass band that had evidently lost their way. Got 'em to play a little concert for us; and before we knew it, that boy was kidnapped right outta here by that Balieu girl. You remember her, don't you, Ella? Lived over there by the church. Just run up here and scooped up that boy on to the back of her horse and run off into the night. Don't know what come over her. She was always so quiet. Never heard a peep out of her."

At the mention of the bluegrass band, I remembered that Leon said Miss Jane had told him that Jubal was traveling with a bluegrass band. "That boy about my size and age?" I asked.

"Oh, I don't rightly remember. He was just a boy, kinda stood off to himself. Didn't play with the band; I remember that. Good band."

"Which way did they go?" I asked.

"The band or the boy and girl? Don't matter. I don't know. Wasn't none of my business."

"How do we get out of here?" I queried. I figured that there would be a limited number of ways for the girl to take the boy who I was almost sure was Jubal.

"Don't know. Never been past the end of the street. 'Course, J.W. knows."

"We go out the same way we came in," replied J.W. "There's no real road. You just drive to the end of the street and keep going 'til you find a path that looks like it goes somewhere; then you follow it. Least that's how we left before."

"Well, let's go," I said anxiously.

We got into the hearse and headed back down the street toward where we had come in the night before. Just before we got to the end of the street, I said, "Wait, turn around! We need to go out the other end of town. We didn't see any sign of them coming in this way; they must have gone out the other way."

"We didn't see anything last night because it was dark," said J.W. "What makes you think they would have gone the other way?"

I realized there was no logic involved in my decision, but I persisted. "I don't know. But what have we got to lose?"

So J.W. turned the hearse around, and we drove back down the street of Longview and straight into the woods. Sure enough, a path emerged that turned into a two-rutted road covered in tall weeds. I looked behind us, and there was no sign of Longview.

Chapter 18

When the phone rang at Miss Jane's house that morning, she rushed to answer it. She had not heard from Leon and Raymond, and she was worried that something might have happened to keep them from bringing Jubal back to Taggart. Assuming it was Leon, she said, "Leon, is Jubal alright?"

"This ain't Leon, Miss Simpson. This is Maybelle Sykes. I figured I better call you and let you know…"

"Is Jubal alright?" she almost shouted into the telephone.

"Well, far as I know, he ain't hurt or nothin'; but I thought you ought to know he run off this mornin'. I tried to talk him out of it, but it didn't do no good. That boy is so in love that there just ain't no reasoning with him. I done…"

"In love! Who's he in love with?"

"She's this girl what showed up here with him and they…"

"He's run away with a girl? Who is she?"

"Well, they run away to get here from someplace they never told me about; then she run off during the fire. Then Jubal, he couldn't stand her bein' gone so he took off after her."

"After the fire? What fire?" Miss Jane was getting more and more excited as Maybelle tried to tell her what had transpired.

"Jubal was in a fire? Did you take him to the hospital?"

"No, ma'am, he wasn't in the fire. The fire burned down my 'bacca barn. Now, he did run out there and try to help me put it out; but it was too much for the two us, and Jenny left while we were trying to put out the fire."

"Jenny is the girl he's in love with?"

"Yes, ma'am."

"Why did she set the fire?"

"No, ma'am, she didn't set the fire. Lightnin' hit the barn and started the fire…"

"Why did she run from the fire then if she didn't set it?"

"Now, just hold on a minute, Miss Simpson. Calm yourself 'fore you have a heart attack or something and I"ll…"

"Where is Jubal? What have you done with him?" shouted Miss Jane.

Maybelle was becoming as exasperated as Miss Jane was upset. In desperation, she said, "Miss Simpson, if you'll just shut the hell up, I'll tell you what you want to know!"

There was a silence. Miss Jane pulled some Kleenex out of a box sitting on the kitchen table, blew her nose and wiped her eyes. Maybelle lit a cigarette.

Then Maybelle told Miss Jane the whole story as best she knew it. "Now, as far as I know, Jubal is okay. He's a smart boy. He just got caught up in a situation that, you know, just seemed to snowball;

and it kinda dimmed his judgment. Marvin Lee—that's my son who's the deputy sheriff here—has gone lookin' for him; and if he's to be found, Marvin Lee will find him. He knows all the fields and woods and near 'bout every knothole around here. Plus, he's got the whole sheriff's department and the Minot Springs police lookin' too."

Miss Jane had calmed down considerably, enough to speak into the phone without shouting, "I do appreciate your calling me, Miss Sykes; and I apologize for being so upset, but you have to realize that Jubal is…" And she starting crying again.

"I know," said Maybelle. "I completely understand how you feel, and that's the reason I wanted to call you. Sometimes the waitin' and not knowin' is worse than knowin', and I can tell you that I believe he's going to be alright.

I hope that's some comfort to you."

"Yes, that is some comfort. And how are Leon and Raymond?"

"I don't know a Leon or Raymond. Who are they?"

"Oh, dear! What has happened to them? Oh, no, no, no!" She began to cry and talk through her tears. "Leon is my fiancé, and Raymond is Jubal's best friend. They should have called by now. Oh, I can't handle this! They left to go pick up Jubal, but I haven't heard from them. I thought it was their call when you called." Then Miss Jane just sobbed without interruption.

Maybelle let her cigarette ash fall unnoticed to the kitchen floor.

Her heart went out to his woman so many miles away. They were different in so many ways; but they shared a mother's concern for her children, an emotion that transcends all differences. She wished there was something she could do, but she knew there was nothing beyond offering consolation. "Now, Miss Simpson, we got to look for the positive here. We don't know what's happened so we just gotta let the Lord take care of it. We just got to keep on going. Now, don't you worry and I'll call you if I hear anything."

After Maybelle hung up the phone, she gazed out the kitchen door to see the still-smoking ashes of her tobacco barn while the sound of Miss Jane's sobs echoed in her ears. "And I think I got problems," she whispered to herself.

Chapter 19

Miss Jane sat at the kitchen table, the phone still in her hand after talking to Maybelle Sykes. Her mind still reeled from the conversation she had just had. She hung up the phone and dried her tears and contemplated her next move. She wasn't going to sit around and wait for the next phone call. There had to be something she could do. She picked up the phone again and dialed Dad's number at the newspaper office. "Ray, have you heard from Raymond or Leon?" she asked.

"No, I haven't and, frankly, I'm beginning to worry about them. What have you heard?"

Miss Jane related the whole story that she had gotten from Maybelle. She was composed and calm as she described the situation. "I'm not going to just sit here and wait, Ray. What can we do?"

My dad was not a man to make hasty decisions. He would consider every detail of a situation and consider every option before acting on anything. He paused briefly, then said, "Let me talk to Chief Gains first and see if he's heard anything; then I'll call you back."

Dad got up from his desk and walked back to the newsroom

where the reporters were busy putting together the next issue of the paper. "Casey," he called to the city editor, "I want you to check the news service wires and see if you can find anything that mentions a young boy and any kind of disturbance. Then send out a notice to every paper you can reach and let them know that we're looking for Jubal Simpson. Give them a description and all that. Do the same thing with Leon McCoy and Raymond, Jr. That hearse ought to stick out like a sore thumb wherever it is. I'm going over to Chief Gain's office. Call me over there if you hear anything."

The police station was just around the corner from the newspaper office, so it only took Dad a few minutes before he was standing in Chief Gains' office. "Chief, we need to find some natives of Taggart who have gone missing. I mean we need to pull out all the stops, use every means available."

"I assume you're taking about Jubal Simpson. I don't know what else to do, Ray. I've sent out missing-person bulletins to all those places you told me, and the county sheriff has looked all over this county for him. I don't know what other resources I can call on."

"How about the National Guard?"

"Well, that might be a stretch. I can't do that, you know. That's up to the governor, and it's got to be a right big deal to even ask him to do that."

"This is a big deal, Chief. Three residents of the Commonwealth of Virginia, the county of Custis and the town of Taggart are missing. One of them is my son. That's a pretty damned big deal if you asked me. John Battle's a friend of mine, and my paper helped get him elected. I believe I can convince him to help, but you have to officially ask him. Get him on the phone. And you might as well call Kerr Scott down in Raleigh. I believe he'll help us too." This was not the well-thought-out, deliberative action expected of Raymond Lovejoy, Sr., the newspaper editor. This was an anxious father and friend.

In about two hours the Virginia National Guard was officially notified that three residents of Taggart were missing. Their descriptions were sent to all units. Dad's conversation with his friend Kerr Scott didn't yield support at first, but a subsequent call from Governor Battle got North Carolina's involvement too. By the next day, a brigade from Greensboro was searching the area.

Dad always told me if you're going to do something, go at it with everything you've got. In the case of looking for us, I believe he followed his own instructions.

Chapter 20

Jubal walked all night. Sometimes the little game trail would disappear into thick brush so he would have to walk around the area until he found another trail. He didn't really know what direction he was going, but he sensed that he was headed in the right way.

He tried to keep his mind from focusing on the strenuous trek. He would imagine he was on some safari in deepest, darkest Africa or winding through the jungles of South America in search of some lost civilization or looking for El Dorado, the city of gold, in Mexico. But the reality always came back. Each step was an intentional move toward finding Jenny. Each step overcame the hunger in his stomach, the thirst in his throat and the soreness of his legs. The image of the jungle not only stirred his imagination but, oddly enough, reminded him of his father. He had heard stories about his father's military service in the south Pacific. Each time he thought of how those islands looked, the pictures in National Geographic and the newsreels, he could picture in his mind the same sight that his father would have seen as he flew his missions.

Of course, he never really got to know his father. Jubal was only ten when his father was killed. But he had the images in the photos that his mother had kept, in the stories she told of how much he had loved his family. He told Mac that he remembered his dad holding the two of them, but Mac always said that was just Jubal's reflection of Mac's memories. Reflection or not, it was a real memory for Jubal. It had only been five years since he died, but it seemed so long ago. There in the woods of North Carolina in the dark of night, in the summer heat and the isolation, he could feel his father's presence. They were sharing an adventure. The heat and the thirst and the weariness were easier to bear. As exhaustion began to take its toll, Jubal felt Jim Simpson lift and carry him through the rhododendron and fir trees, over the ditches and up the hills strewn with pine needles. "Come on, son, we can do this," came the voice through the night. "We Simpson men are always up to the challenge. We never give up." Jubal knew he was no longer alone.

And when Jubal awoke to daylight, he found himself beside a little mountain stream, a narrow, clear, cool trickle that slid over some tan rocks on its way down hill. He rolled over on his side and put his face in the stream, gulping the water as it washed his face. Then he turned and looked up at the sky through the trees. The sun was at an angle. That meant that it is was sometime after noon, but he had no idea exactly what time it was or where he was. The sun rays spread to the floor of the woods through the trees. Shadows filled in between the rays and the tree limbs, cutting across the light. Jubal felt like he might be in the bottom of some giant woven basket.

He heard the rustle of leaves behind him and turned, thinking it was a bird or some animal searching for food. But it wasn't. It was Prince Albert Walker. "You are a valiant warrior, Jubal Simpson," said the giant black man as he approached Jubal there by the little stream. "A warrior, a boy who has become a man, a man who has found himself while searching for someone else." The Prince was still clad in the same clothes he had been wearing when Jubal last saw him as he performed for him and the band members at the cabin. He still wore the bib overalls and flannel shirt and the old shapeless felt hat covered his head. But he had added an incongruous element to his costume. He wore a big, flowing black cape with red lining.

Sensing Jubal's curiosity, the Prince said, "A carryover from my earlier days." Jubal thought, *One more piece of mystery.*

Jubal wasn't surprised to see his old acquaintance. He wasn't expecting to find him; but he somehow knew that if he were to find Jenny, Prince Albert would have something to do with it.

The big man reached out his hand to help Jubal rise from the side of the stream. Jubal took it without hesitation and asked, "Where is Jenny?"

The big man laughed as he said, "Ah, a man of single purpose. What makes you think I know where she is?"

"Past experience. You seem to know where everything and everybody is," answered Jubal. "Will you take me to her?"

"What if I said 'no'?"

"I will keep searching until I find her."

"And that is why I will take you to her. Follow me," he instructed.

Jubal did as he was instructed. The Prince set a fast pace, but Jubal didn't seem to mind despite the fatigue of his journey. He was excited, exhilarated and anxious to see Jenny, to talk to her, to find out why she had run away.

They proceeded through the woods on no apparent path without any deviation in the direction. No impediments slowed their progress, and it seemed to Jubal that they had only gone a fairly short distance before he saw the familiar cabin. The heat of the day had not abated, but smoke arose from the chimney of the cabin. Jubal figured that meant the cook stove was fired up and that food would soon be available. As they got closer to the cabin, the sound of piano music lifted from the cabin like the smoke from the chimney. Jenny was there! He began to run toward the cabin, but the Prince reached out his big hand and grasped his arm as he started to run. "Wait here," he said as the two of them stood still only a few yards from the cabin. "Always look at what you see, boy. Look with more than your eyes. Within your vision there will always be more than things, more than objects. Everything you see, hear, touch will become a part of who you are. Soak it all in; paint the picture in your mind using your senses as the brush, leave out nothing so that when the time comes to recall each moment in your life, there will be a full canvas."

So they stood there in the sunlight and smelled the smoke from the cook stove and listened to the music and felt the soft breeze caress their skin while the colors and shapes of the land and the buildings soaked through them. That moment before he was to see Jenny again would become a part of his soul.

That perceptive interlude calmed Jubal, but it didn't erase the anticipation of seeing Jenny. When he opened the door of the cabin, he saw her at the piano. His first reaction was that she looked older somehow. Maybe it was her hair. Gone was the ponytail, and in its place was a soft coiffure that let the ends kind of turn up at the bottom and float just above her shoulders. And she wore a dress. It was just a simple little white cotton dress with blue polka dots. Gone were the tennis shoes, and in their place was a pair of white socks inside black-and-white saddle oxfords. She stopped playing the piano, smiled and said, "Hey, Jubal."

He needed no prompting to stop and take it all in. But in the course of absorbing the scene before him and seeing the change in Jenny, Jubal was jolted into looking at himself. Mud and sweat still covered him; and he abruptly turned, looking for the Prince to ask where he could clean up. But the Prince was nowhere to be seen. So the first words he spoke to Jenny after his toilsome journey and all the longing thoughts that had gone through his mind were, "You're beautiful and I look like hell, don't I?"

Jenny laughed and said, "No, I think you look wonderful; but I I'm sure you don't feel wonderful. There's a bathroom with a shower right through the kitchen and through the door. When you get cleaned up, we'll talk."

Jubal found the bathroom, shed his dirty clothes and got in the shower. He let the water run over his body, washing away not just the mud and sweat but also the fatigue of his journey and the weight of not knowing where Jenny was. When he emerged from the shower, he found his clothes, cleaned and lying on the floor. *How'd he do that?* he asked himself. *Another mystery in the world of Prince Albert Watson* was the silent answer.

He could hear Jenny playing the piano as he got dressed. The music sounded familiar, but he couldn't remember exactly where he had heard it.

"Rachmaninoff," said Prince Albert as Jubal walked back into the kitchen.

"What?" Jubal asked in surprise.

"Not *what... who.* You were wondering where you had heard that music before. It's a composition by Sergei Rachmaninoff, a Russian composer. You heard me play it upon the occasion of your previous visit. Jenny plays it better than I do."

And he reads minds too, thought Jubal.

The smell of fried chicken cooking on the wood-burning stove brought back memories of meals at home back in Taggart. Mama's meals. "Mama! She must be worried to death about me. I've got to get in touch with her," he said out loud.

"We'll call her in a little while," said Prince Albert. "Right now you need to get reacquainted."

Just as before, Prince Albert set a simple but elegant table that exceeded the more modest fare of the previous visit: fried chicken with mashed potatoes and gravy and green beans and, of course, the best vintage clear water.

Jenny joined him at the table in the kitchen as Prince Albert served the meal. Then he disappeared and the two young people talked. They talked about what had happened to both of them together and separately in the relatively short time they had known each other. They talked about the band, the ride to Maybelle's and the fire; and then, when it got to the point of talking about the future,

Jubal said, "When we get back to Taggart..."

"I'm not going to Taggart, Jubal. That's not the place for me. There's a whole big world out there that I have only visited. I want to see and be a part of it. Prince Albert has been my mentor. He taught me to play the piano, and I want to take that enhanced gift wherever I can. He can help me make the transition. My whole life, or at least the part I can remember, has been limited to Longview and, frankly, I don't even know if that is a real world. I do know I want to know what is beyond my limited past and even more limited present. Until you came along, I never thought beyond Longview, beyond the present. You changed my life and I am... I am grateful. That's what I kept thinking about at Miss Maybelle's, that if my life could change so quickly in the short time I had known you and you had such an effect on me, what would my life be like if I went other places and met more people, explored… explored me and found out there was more to me than just you. That is why I ran away at Miss Maybelle's. I wasn't running away from you. I was running to me."

Jenny had spoken bluntly and unemotionally, but Jubal's emotions heard what she said and so he heard something different. The idea that they were not going to be together had never entered his mind. In his mind he would find Jenny and they would go back to Taggart and… and live happily ever after. In that moment Jubal realized that he had not really looked at things in a logical way, in a mature way, the way a grown-up would look at things. Just as his romanticized idea of going off to fight a war with his brother was illogical and unrealistic in retrospect, so was his concept of life with Jenny. That realization didn't make it any easier to accept, and he kept thinking of ways to reconcile his past and new perceptions.

"I'll go with you," he said desperately.

"And what would you do? You wouldn't be satisfied with a life in which you would be... you would be peripheral."

"Peripheral? What does that mean?" he asked.

"It means you'd be on the edge, and eventually we would grow so apart you would be on the outside and that… that would break my heart. If I go on now and you go back to Taggart and get on with your life, we will always be a part of each other, don't you see?

We'll be like a flower with two blossoms… always together but growing and becoming beautiful separately."

Jubal understood Jenny's logic; he even understood the flower analogy, but it didn't make it any easier to accept what she was saying. "Maybe someday I'll think you're right, but not today," he said.

He abruptly got up from the table and walked outside. He looked up at the moonless sky and felt the tiniest raindrop fall on his face. Maybe it wasn't a raindrop. Coulda been a tear.

"Time to call your mother," said Prince Albert as he walked up behind Jubal standing there in the dark… alone.

He put his hand on Jubal's shoulder and turned them toward the woods beside the barn. The darkness of the night deepened the gloom of the woods as they approached it. Jubal was still trying to process all that had happened to him back in the cabin. "Wait!" he said. "I have to go back."

"No, you don't," said Prince Albert. "There's nothing you can say that she doesn't already know."

Chapter 21

The path that J.W. chose to follow through the woods after we left Longview was random, to say the least. I don't know if it was ever a road because there was so little to mark it; just the fact that some weeds were higher in some places than others was about the only indication that maybe someone or something had been there previously. The fact that a heavy fog had settled on the landscape didn't help either.

"You have no idea where we're going, do you?" asked Ella.

"Of course not," answered J.W. "That's the fun of it, the challenge, the adventure! Where's the excitement of knowing where you're going? That's why we left Longview the first time if you remember. Back there we knew that every day would be like the day before. Life is too precious to be ordinary. We've got to press on to the unknown, grasp the unfamiliar and, above all, embrace the mysterious!"

"Define the indefinite, unveil the anonymous!" chimed in Ella with a laugh as she looked toward me sitting between the two of them. "You don't seem to share our enthusiasm for this journey, Raymond. What's the matter?" she asked.

"Well, frankly, I've got a lot of unfinished business to take care of before I can share your sense of freedom from responsibility," I said condescendingly. Suddenly I felt like I was the adult sitting between two children. I was conflicted. Almost unwillingly I wanted to go on some kind of great adventure with my new friends, leave my ordinary life, slip the bonds of conformity and absorb the wider world. At the same time, my sense of loyalty to my friends and family back home and my sense of responsibility to do what was expected of me outweighed my fantasy. As soon as I had said it, I was sorry. "I'm sorry," I said. "I didn't mean to throw a wet blanket on the party. It's just that I really need to find Leon and take Jubal back home. Besides, I know that my dad is worried about me and I…I need to…"

All at once the weight of my circumstances overwhelmed me. I didn't cry, but I wanted to. I wanted things to be like they had been. I wanted to be comfortable and secure and certain of things. In view of everything, I concluded that adventure was greatly overrated.

"You're right. First things first," said Ella as she put her arm around my shoulder. "We're going to find your friend and get you back on your trip. Unfortunately, we don't exactly know how we're going to do that right now, but let's be optimistic and believe that it will happen."

As if on cue, the fog lifted and we could see ahead more clearly. There was an actual road before us, at least more of a road than we had been on. Two parallel paths created a winding road through what appeared to be a young forest of pine trees planted in rows… a field of trees.

"See those young trees, Jubal?" said J.W. "They are a good sign. That new forest means that at some time or other, the old forest left, probably burned up or logged out, but somebody—some human— came along and planted a new forest. Now, it might have been another human that set the fire or cut the trees, but you gotta also believe another human came along to replace the trees. Remember that the next time you think the world is going to hell in a hand basket. For every bad person that does something bad, there's a good person that does something good. I had to learn that the hard way. So now you know, and you don't have to learn the hard way." Then he laughed that big laugh and said, "Life is good, my boy! Life is good! Remember that."

The appearance of a real road lifted my spirits immediately. The fact that we didn't know where it led only slightly tempered my elation.

As we rounded a curve, we saw an intersection ahead. Immediately I knew that meant we were going to have to choose in what direction we would continue our search for Leon. But then I saw that my concern was unfounded. At the intersection lay the remains of an old building that had burnt to the ground long ago.

There was a sign where the roads came together that read "Prince Albert" and on the other side of the road, sitting on a picnic table, was Leon.

"There he is!" I shouted. "Right there! Right there!"

Before J.W. could stop the hearse, I was scrambling to get over

201

Ella to open the door. She said, "Just wait a minute and I'll get out of your way." As soon as the door swung open, I was out of the hearse; my hands hit the ground first, but I jumped to my feet and ran to Leon. He was standing by the picnic table as I grabbed him and hugged him. I don't know if my reaction was so much because I cared that much about Leon or that I knew that finding him was the next step to getting back home.

"Leon, where have you been?" I shouted at him as if the louder my voice, the quicker and more understandable the explanation. He was wearing the same tan suit, white shirt and red tie he was wearing when he ran off the road in the rainstorm.

"Damned if I know," he answered flatly. "All I know is when we slipped off the road back yonder, I figured somebody would come along to get us back on; and I didn't want to get out in the rain to wait for 'em so I just figured I'd take a nap 'til they got there. Next thing I know I'm sleeping on a picnic table in the middle of nowhere, and you show up with two people driving a hearse."

"How long have you been waiting," I asked.

"Oh, I haven't been waiting long, I don't think. I woke up just before I saw y'all coming around that curve. You got any idea where we are?"

"Nope, but that sign over there says 'Prince Albert.' I don't know if that's the name of this place or not, but the name is definitely familiar."

As we were talking, J.W. and Ella joined us. "This is J.W. and Ella," I said. "They picked me up back there when we ran off the road." I started to explain who they were and what had transpired since they picked me up, but realized that I still didn't know much about them and what we had experienced together was way too complicated to try to explain to Leon right then.

"Really glad to meet you, Leon," said J.W. as he shook hands with Leon. "You've got a real friend in Raymond here. He never gave up looking for you."

"We apologize for the little dent on the door of your hearse. That happened when we literally ran into you back during the rainstorm," said Ella as she too shook hands with Leon.

Leon looked over at the hearse and said, "Must have been a very small car and a very soft crash. I can hardly see the dent from here."

"Well, it wasn't a car and it wasn't really a crash. We were on a bicycle and just kinda slid into you," she said.

At the mention of the bicycle, J.W. said, "That reminds me, Ella. Now that we've reunited Raymond and Leon, we can proceed on our quest."

"Our quest to nowhere," she said as she looked at me, reminding me of the philosophy of life they had imparted to me in the relatively short period of our acquaintance.

J.W. walked over to the hearse, opened the back and removed the bicycle. He closed the back door, pushed the bicycle over to where we were standing and the two of them got on and immediately began to ride off.

"Hey, wait!" I shouted after them. "Where are you going?"

"Away," said Ella as she waved back at us and quickly disappeared around the curve in the road.

"Boy, that's a strange pair," murmured Leon.

"So are we," I said as I looked down the empty road.

Chapter 22

Jubal and Prince Albert had not spoken since leaving the cabin that night. Jubal was still trying to sort out all that had happened to him and wondering what was ahead. He walked resignedly behind Prince Albert, heedless of the direction they were going. Their path was narrow and up and down hills covered with fir trees and rhododendron and a wide variety of other plants. The night covered everything around them, but he hardly noticed his surroundings.

Their trek was unlike the one that had led him from Maybelle's to Prince Albert's cabin. There was no sun to heat the cool night air and he wasn't thirsty or hungry, but he did feel tired. The short time he had spent at Prince Albert's cabin had not been restful. The shower and the food had provided a temporary rejuvenation, but Jenny's revelation of her intent far outweighed the benefit of the respite.

So they plodded along into the night until they came to a little meadow. As he looked over his shoulder back toward Jenny and the cabin, he saw a half-moon grazing the top of the hills. Then as he turned again to follow Prince Albert, he saw the sunrise ahead of them. Somehow, he thought, the scene was appropriate. As beautiful as the past with Jenny had been, he knew that the future held great promise because he had learned so much. They paused there in the meadow, the boy who had become a man and the mysterious man who had been the conduit for much of the transformation. They stood there for a long time without speaking; then Prince Albert said, "In just a short time now, I'm going to leave you. We will never meet again; and if you choose to tell anyone about me, they will not believe you. But I want to give you this as a parting gift." He handed Jubal a piece of stiff, brown leather about the size of an ordinary business card. Stamped into the leather was the name "Leonidas J. Godfrey, Esq.," nothing else. "Keep it. Don't lose it," he instructed as he turned and resumed their trek.

Chapter 23

"Is Prince Albert a person, a place or a thing?" asked Leon as he gestured toward the sign on the other side of the road.

"Yes," I answered.

"That wasn't a yes-or-no question," pointed out Leon.

"Well, I don't really know," I replied. "You see, I keep hearing that name, but nobody has ever told me who he is. Now here we see a sign with his name on it, but it's not pointing in any direction; and there's nothing here but a burnt building, a picnic table and… and a phone booth." I had not noticed the phone booth before but immediately ran over to it. "We gotta call Miss Jane and Dad," I said as I took the receiver off the hook and dialed "0." When the operator answered, I said, "I need to place a collect call to TA3-3954 in Taggart, Virginia."

The phone only rang once before Miss Jane answered it. "Yes!" she shouted into the receiver.

"You have a collect call from…" said the operator before she was interrupted by Miss Jane.

"Lord, yes!! Jubal, are you alright?" she immediately asked.

"This is Raymond, Miss Jane. I wanted to call…"

"Are y'all alright?"

"Yes, ma'am, far as I know. I..."

"Let me speak to Jubal."

"Well, he's not here right now, but..."

"Yes, I am," came the voice from behind me. "Let me talk to Mama."

I turned to see Jubal walking across the road from the picnic table area. I was so surprised I couldn't speak as he came over and took the phone out of my hand. "Hello, Mama," he said. "We're alright. We're on our way home right now."

"Where are you?"

"Well, I don't know exactly. We had some car trouble, and we stopped at a place called Prince Albert; but we're going to get back on the road right now," he said as he looked at me and Leon in amazement.

"Where in the world have y'all been? Ray and I have been worried to death about you. He's notified every newspaper in North Carolina and Virginia; and the police and highway patrol in both states are looking for you, not to mention the National Guard."

"The National Guard?" said Jubal incredulously. "The National Guard's out looking for us? Oh, shit!"

Panic shown in all our faces as we grasped the extent of what was happening. "Look, Mama, tell Mr. Ray to call off the National Guard and the police and all that. We're alright and we're on the way home, and we'll call you as soon as we get to another phone. I love you," he said and quickly hung up the phone.

"We gotta go," Jubal ordered as he hung up the phone and we all headed for the hearse. Leon got behind the wheel, started the engine, pushed in the clutch and hesitated. "Which way do we go?" he asked.

"That way. That's the way Prince Albert told me," he said as he indicated a road that looked to me just like the others. But I didn't question him right then about Prince Albert or his directions.

Leon shifted the big hearse into gear and spun it around in the middle of the intersection. None of us said a word as we sped down the dirt road, leaving a cloud of dust behind us. We splattered mud holes and straddled ruts in the road, not even looking at the landscape around us. It looked all the same: miles and miles of short pine trees.

Shortly we saw what appeared to be a large cloud of dust at some distance down the road directly ahead of us. "That's probably the National Guard coming for us," said Jubal. "Oh, Lord. We are going to jail," he said. "Just because I had a crazy idea of going to war with my brother. Stupid, stupid."

Neither Leon nor I disagreed with him or offered to make him feel any better. We figured we were all going to jail because we had gotten the police and the National Guard in two states out looking for us. They'd probably make us reimburse them for the cost of searching for us before they sent us to jail.

"Maybe we can outrun them and get back to Taggart before they do and just explain it was all a mistake," said Leon. Leon was the oldest member of our trio of miscreants, and he was talking like we were in some Roy Rogers movie where the young cowboy or cowgirl was always forgiven for whatever mischief they had caused.

But this was no Saturday-afternoon matinee.

"Nope, we'll just go on and take our punishment and move on," said Jubal. "That's what you do when something like this happens. You just keep on going."

The dust cloud seemed to be getting bigger and bigger. "Must be a lotta folks in that crowd," I observed. Then the realization hit me. That wasn't a cloud of dust; it was smoke.

My two companions came to the same realization at the same time. "That is not dust," said Leon. "That's smoke. Must be a big forest fire up there." He stopped the hearse and we all got out and stood in the road, looking toward the smoke. We could smell it. The wind was bearing the smoke our way. That meant the fire was coming our way too.

"What you think we ought to do? Turn around and try to outrun it? You reckon there could be another road off this one either behind us on in front of us?" queried Leon.

"It's moving too fast for us to outrun it; and as big as it looks, any roads off it will be in its path too," said Jubal.

"So what do you suggest, O Wise One?" I said sarcastically.

"This is the way we need to go. Straight ahead. We just keep on going," he answered.

So we got back in the hearse. This time I crawled in the back and lay down on the bed of the hearse, the place where they put the coffins. I figured Leon didn't need me jamming him up if he were going to try to steer through a forest fire.

We had all the windows rolled up, but the smell of the smoke was getting stronger. We could see that it was getting thicker, and Leon could not see the edge of the road.

"This is a straight road," observed Leon. "There have been some hills, but there hasn't been a curve in it since we left that intersection," he said. "As strong as that wind's blowing, the fire's probably moving pretty fast and burning everything behind it clean. The short trees don't have limbs long enough to fall across the road. Just gotta hold it in the middle." And with that conviction, Leon slammed his foot to the gas pedal and we proceeded into the thick smoke.

I couldn't really tell how fast we were going; and I didn't dare try to look over Leon's shoulder at the speedometer, but I knew it was fast. Leon had a tight grip on the steering wheel, not letting it move in either direction. Every few seconds I would see flames lick at the side of the hearse as the heat rose steadily inside its confines. My clothes were wet with sweat; and every breath I took was hot, the smoke filling my nostrils until I thought I was not going to be able to take another breath.

Then suddenly we broke through the heavy smoke. Small puffs of smoke still emerged from the stumps that remained in the tree fields on each side of the road. They were now just little more than vapors, tiny contrails that rose straight into the air, remnants of an inferno. Leon slowed the hearse as we proceeded down the road. In my smoke-clouded mind, the still-burning tree stumps were torches lining the way as we made a triumphal re-entry into the world. We had run the gauntlet and emerged victorious.

Leon and Jubal rolled the windows down, and a relatively cool breeze blew through. It was still hot and smoky, but the intensity was much less. A few more miles and Leon stopped in the middle of the road, and we again got out of the car.

We didn't say anything. We just stood there and looked behind us as we saw the big cloud of smoke still consuming the small trees like a flaming combine. All around us was grey with only a few sprinkles of red. No trees to the horizon.

I looked over at Leon. He was not the same Leon with whom I had left Taggart. He was not the guy we took for granted, Miss Jane's beau, the nerd, that little guy down at the funeral home. He was a hero. He was our knight in smoky armor.

I went over to him and, for the second time that day, hugged him. Then Jubal did the same. "The Three Musketeers, that's what we are," said Leon, trying to keep things from becoming maudlin.

A good analogy, I thought as we all laughed and shook off the awkward moment.

The ominous wail of sirens made us all turn to look down the road ahead. In a few seconds, we saw a real cloud of dust coming our way.

"National Guard?" I wondered out loud.

"Nope. Fire trucks," said Jubal.

We quickly got back in the hearse, and Leon maneuvered it to the side of the road as the fire trucks sped by us. After they had passed, I felt a certain amount of relief. What could have been a tragedy had been averted, and we were finally on the way home. Behind us were acres of what had been a re-emerging forest. It could be revived with enough rain and sunshine. But what about Longview?

Chapter 24

We had been riding only a few minutes after the fire trucks passed us before we came to a paved road. None of us knew exactly where we were; but after some rudimentary calculations based primarily on conjecture, we decided that left was north and we wanted to go north. So we turned left onto the paved road.

The jostle of the dirt road changed to the steady hum of the pavement that almost seemed to hypnotize us. No one spoke or thought to turn the radio on to break the soothing peacefulness that swept over us. We were all lost in our own thoughts.

As I thought back over my own experiences of the previous days, I thought again about that Prince Albert that I had heard about. J.W., Ella and Miss Arlene had mentioned him, and then that sign had shown up and Jubal had gotten the direction to go home from the same fellow.

"Hey, Jubal," I said, breaking the silence. "Who's that Prince Albert you were going to tell us about?"

Jubal didn't answer right away. After some contemplation, he said, "Oh, just some guy I met. Don't know much about him, and you wouldn't believe me if I told you." Then quickly changing the subject, he said, "Hey, don't forget that we got to stop and call

Mama as soon as we get to a phone booth." Then he reached over and turned on the radio. He turned the dial through a lot of static before settling on a country-music station.

"I didn't know you liked country music," said Leon.

"I don't particularly, but I thought I might pick up some guys I met a couple of days ago. Pretty good bluegrass band. Met 'em when I was catching a ride with a traveling preacher."

"You been traveling with a preacher?" I asked. That started Jubal's recitation of his travels. Leon and I listened without interrupting him as he told us about Reverend Branson and Billy and the bluegrass band, the tent fire and how he had convinced them to use moonshine for gasoline. "…and we wound up right back there where we just left, there at the picnic stand."

"You been there all that time?" I asked.

"Well, not exactly," he said. "Hey, there's a phone booth!" he shouted, pointing to a booth beside a small country store, the first building we had seen for several miles.

Leon swerved the hearse over onto the dirt area in front of the store without even slowing down. He spewed dust and gravel against the gas pump before he came to a halt beside it. We had barely stopped before Jubal got out of the car and ran to the phone booth. Leon and I got out and Leon asked, "You got any money?"

"Yeah, a little bit, I think." I reached in my pocket and finally came up with a few coins and handed them to Leon. Leon searched his pockets and by combining our meager financial resources, we came up with almost two dollars. I heard the screen door of the country store slam and turned to see a boy about the same age as me and Jubal come walking toward us.

"I reckon y'all want some gas, don't ya?" he asked.

"Yes, two dollars' worth, please," responded Leon.

As the boy came around to pump the gas, he said, "Y'all must be in some kind of a hurry the way you come flyin' in here throwin' rocks up against the store like that. You rob a bank?" Evidently the boy thought himself quite a wit as he laughed loud and long at his comment.

"If we had robbed a bank, we'd have more than two dollars between us." I stated the figure not so much for his information as just a realization of our situation.

"Where are we?" I inquired of our comedic attendant.

"You at my daddy's store. Says so right there on the Co-Cola sign. Says 'Godfrey's Store' right there plain as day." Again, he laughed at his own humor.

"Are there any other smart people in the store?" asked Leon.

The boy evidently missed Leon's sarcasm as he replied earnestly, "Nope, just me."

Leon and I went into the store and were surprised to find a man seated on a wooden stool behind the counter which ran the length of the little building. He wore a pair of khaki pants and a khaki shirt, and on his feet were what my father called "brogans," high-topped leather shoes.

In one corner of the little store was a square metal drum with a hand pump attached to dispense kerosene. On the other side were several wooden baskets filled with vegetables, all placed in a row under a table on which a variety of snacks had been stacked. Against the other wall was a red box cooler that gurgled with cool water that circulated around some bottled soft drinks placed in the bottom. Even the smell of the kerosene only slightly diluted the effect of the sight of such items.

"Y'all look like you could be a mite hungry," said the man on the stool.

"As a matter of fact, we haven't had anything for a while," I said.

"Well, I believe that if a man's thirsty, we should give him drink; and if he's hungry, we should feed him. Says something like that in the Bible. Help yourself," directed the man.

Leon and I walked over and picked up a honey bun each, plus one for Jubal and pulled three Coca-Colas out of the cooler.

"Something for our friend outside, if that's alright?" I asked meekly. There was something about this man that made me like him immediately, an affection acquired almost as quickly as the disdain for the gas attendant.

"Certainly," he said. "Where y'all headed?"

217

"A place you've probably never heard of: Taggart, Virginia," I replied.

"Oh, yeah. I heard of it. Matter of fact, got some family up there. You might know 'em. Aaron and Helen Gravely. Married my mama's cousin, Aaron did. Think they got a buncha young'uns probably 'bout your age, I reckon. Now, what was your name?"

"I'm Raymond Lovejoy, Jr. and this is my friend, Leon McCoy," I said.

"Nice to meet you fellas. You know, come to think of it, I was in the Army with a fellow from there too. Good man. Got killed during the war."

I immediately thought, *What a coincidence! Could this man have known Jubal's father.* I had to ask, "His name wasn't Simpson, was it?"

"Nope. Name was Leroy Montgomery. Buried him on a little farm outside Paris. I was right beside him when he died. Used to talk a lot about Taggart. Seemed to be a nice town."

"You wouldn't happen to know how to get to Taggart from here, would you?" I asked.

"Sure do. You just go on up this road you're on right here and turn left on the next paved road before you get to Councilman's Dairy. Take you straight into Taggart. 'Bout ten miles."

Ten miles! Ten miles from home. I had no idea how many miles we had traveled individually or collectively in the past few days, but it really didn't matter. We were just ten miles from home.

"Hey, guess what, y'all? Mac's back home!" shouted Jubal as he ran into the store. "Mama said they turned him down because he had a heart murmur. Didn't know there was anything wrong with his heart, but I'm sure glad they found it. Yep, he's already back home! Come on, let's go!"

He turned around and immediately headed back out the door and toward the hearse. Leon and I rushed to follow him. "Hey, don't forget Jubal's stuff here!" called the man in the store as he followed us out the door and handed us the honey bun and the Coca-Cola.

The three of us jumped in the front seat of the hearse and sped off, again spraying gravel and dirt toward the store. We were too excited to talk, but one thought occurred to me as we turned on the road leading to Taggart: *How did the man know Jubal's name?*

Chapter 25

The reunion in Taggart was a big deal. When we drove up in front of Miss Jane's house, there was a big crowd of people there. I don't know how news spread so fast or exactly why so many people cared that we were back, but it was nice to see. Of course, Miss Jane ran out to the car and hugged Jubal so hard he almost couldn't breathe, and then she did the same to Leon. My dad was there too. Ordinarily he is a very reserved man. When I got out of the hearse, he walked over to me and said, "I'm sure glad you're home, son," as he reached out to shake my hand; but then he put both arms around me and hugged me like I hadn't been hugged since Mama died.

Then I saw Mac come out on the porch. He didn't look any different from what he had looked when he left to go to Fort Bragg. He was dressed much like he always was: a short-sleeved, white shirt tucked into a pair of blue jeans with the cuffs rolled up above a pair of penny loafers. It was kind of a uniform, but not military. He had that silly grin that was unique to him, kind of a cross between a smile and a full-blown laugh. Jubal ran over to him, up the steps, then jumped up on him, his legs around his waist and his arms around his neck, almost knocking him down.

Then Leon and I walked into the house with Miss Jane and Dad as Jubal and Mac followed. Miss Jane assigned seats. She sat on the couch between Mac and Jubal, Dad and I sat in the chairs on each side of the fireplace and Leon pulled a chair from the dining room and sat at the end of the couch.

For just a few seconds, nobody said anything; then Miss Jane said, "Jubal, you know that you are grounded for the next two weeks." More silence followed.

Then Dad said, "Now, Jane, might we suspend that sentence if he promises to write out his story for the newspaper. I think it would be of interest to everyone in town and a great exercise in journalism. In fact, a collaboration between Jubal and Raymond would be good training for both of them, don't you think?"

After some hesitation, Miss Jane said, "Well, I guess that would be appropriate, given the tremendous interest you have generated with your misbehavior."

Before we could get into much more conversation, the house began to fill up with neighbors and food. Again, I wondered how all this could happen in such a short time. I posed the question to Dad and his response was, "Son, never underestimate the resourcefulness of women in a small town. They can create something wonderful out of practically nothing in almost no time. A group of caring neighbors is a force more powerful than mass armies."

I also asked him about what happened to the National Guard that was out looking for us. "Well," Dad said sheepishly, "the National Guard never did actually go out looking for you. But I did call both governors and cashed in all my political chips as editor of the paper, but Governor Battle was right; it might have been a state of emergency for me, but it wasn't for the state."

I thought that the fact that my dad had even considered such drastic action because I might be in danger said more about him and me than anything he could ever say or write directly to me. I was proud to be a junior.

So over the next few weeks, Jubal and I recounted our adventures for the newspaper. But not everything. Some things we mutually agreed would be best not to tell, specifically about Prince Albert Watson and Jenny. After Jubal told me about her, we both agreed that her role in our story was too personal to share with the public. We asked Leon to tell us about his time between running off the road and appearing at the picnic table, and he had no explanation. So we left that out too. In fact, we decided that we would not necessarily tell the story as it actually happened but would add and subtract according to what we thought would make the most interesting story. We would save the truth for later.

Chapter 26

It wasn't long before the interest in our odyssey dwindled. Everything in Taggart got pretty much back to normal. Mac met a girl at Clarence Newman's wedding named Leanne Whitehurst, whose daddy ran the State Farm Insurance agency over in Martinsville. Mr. Whitehurst decided to set up an office in Taggart so Mac went to work selling insurance.

Miss Jane and Leon officially announced their engagement to get married, but they didn't set a date. Leon gave her a ring that he had been saving up for. Mr. Clanton down at The Jewel Shoppe let him have it at a considerable discount since Leon had given Mr. Clanton a reduced price on the casket for his wife's funeral the year before.

And Jubal and I went back to school. The story we wrote for the newspaper seemed to satisfy our friends. Miss Caroline Canady, our English teacher, said we didn't have to write an essay on what we did on our summer vacation; the newspaper story would suffice. But she did tell Jubal that he had a real talent for writing. I think she was thinking about news reporting, not fiction; but Jubal took her encouragement to heart and began to think about a career as a writer. I had already decided that I was going to journalism school and then come back to work with Dad at the paper so we shared many of the same classes. Our celebrity status in Taggart was temporary, and we all settled back into our familiar lives.

Over the next couple of years, Jubal and I would occasionally talk about our journey; but we, like the rest of the community, put that behind us. It wasn't until we started thinking about leaving Taggart for college that those days came back to us.

Although Miss Jane and Leon had gotten married by then, the financial situation concerning Jubal's college expenses had not changed from what it had been when Mac was considering the same move. Money was tight. Then one spring afternoon I got a call from Jubal to come over to his house right away. He seemed anxious.

"What's the matter?" I asked.

"I got a strange letter this afternoon. I want you to look at it," he responded.

When I got there, he was sitting in the swing that hung on one end of the porch. I walked over to that end of the porch and sat down in the wicker chair. "Whatcha got?" I asked.

He handed me a letter written on official-looking stationery.

The engraved letterhead read "Office of Leonidas J. Godfrey, Esq. Attorney at Law." I noted that the paper quality was expensive. Working in the job on the printing side of the newspaper office had taught me a lot about paper texture and weight. This piece had a watermark that stated it was twenty-four- pound cotton stock, the kind you would use for the most expensive stationery. It was addressed to

Mr. Jubal Early Simpson
313 Waverly Street Taggart, Virginia.
   It read:
Dear Mr. Simpson:

   I am writing to inform you that I have been directed to deposit $5000 in your account at The Bank of Taggart. These funds are to be used solely for the purpose of providing the financial support for your education at whatever college or university you choose. Such expenses shall include tuition, fees, books, room and board and whatever other miscellaneous expenses may occur as a part of the educational process. If a circumstance should arise in which you should require more than this, you will not be able to contact me; but I will be notified and will provide the needed funds. A similar amount will be provided in the same manner and for the same purpose each year at this time for as long as you are a full-time student. Misuse of these funds could result in serious consequences.

Best Regards,
Leonidas J. Godfrey, Esq.

   Of course, my first question was, "Who is Leonidas J.

Godfrey?"

"I have no idea," replied Jubal. "As far as I know, I don't have any kin people by that name. Miss Canady did help me fill out some requests for financial aid when I sent off my college applications, but I don't remember this name; and there's no indication that he is connected with any of the places I applied. And, what's even more curious, I haven't been accepted anywhere yet."

"Have you told Miss Jane yet?"

"No. She'll have the same questions we got, and I can't give her any answers. And you know Mama, she'll start calling all over the place and getting everybody involved; and she's liable to send Leon out looking for Mr. Godfrey. Leon'll do anything Mama asks."

"And we'll be back on the road to another adventure," I laughed. At the mention of our almost-forgotten escapade of a couple of years earlier, the name "Godfrey" flashed through my mind.

"Hey, you remember the little store we stopped at just before we got back to Taggart? Wasn't that named Godfrey's Store or something like that?"

"Oh, yeah. The guy pumping gas pointed it out to us. I remember now. But to be sure, he's not Leonidas J. Godfrey. That man was no lawyer."

"But he could have been kin. And you remember when we left the store, he told me and Leon not to forget your snacks. Called you by name. We never said your name, remember?"

It didn't take much more discussion for us to decide we needed to go back to the old store. Since Jubal and I had periodically been writing stories for the paper, I told Dad that we were going to check on an old store for a possible feature story and asked if we could use his car. After giving us explicit instructions to be back before dark, we left the next Saturday morning and headed back to find the old store.

We drove along the road in silence. We both realized that, for whatever reason, neither of us had been back this way since our passage two years before. This time Leon was not with us; and, instead of rushing back home, we were driving away.

The road ran right up to a junction with another paved road. We saw a billboard in front of us that indicated Councilman's Dairy was down the road to the left. We took a right and soon recognized the road we had been on as we had hurried back to Taggart.

A few miles further and we saw it. There was an old store on the left, but it seemed to have been abandoned. As we pulled up in front of the old rusted gasoline pump, we looked up at the sign above the door to the store. There was the faded lettering between two fading Coca-Cola logos: "Godfrey's Store." The rest of the store was much like the sign, weathered and leaning a little. The screen door was hanging on one hinge, and a padlock held the wooden entrance together. The one window was so covered in dirt we couldn't see the inside.

We walked around the side and behind the store. There was no

227

sign that the store had been in use any time recently. Vines had grown up on both sides of the building and were creeping across the tin roof. Grass and weeds obscured the back of the store, and rust coved an old oil drum that had fallen from its rack against the building.

Jubal and I walked back to the front of the store and looked back at it. "That's a shame. Must have gone broke or something. 'Course, if he gave away all his merchandise to folks like he did us, he didn't make much money."

"Y'all didn't pay for the snacks?" Jubal asked.

"Nope. After we pooled all of our pocket change for the gasoline, we didn't have enough for anything else. The man felt sorry for us, I guess. Told us to help ourselves so we got some for us and for you. Really nice of him. That was while you were on the phone to Miss Jane."

At the mention of the phone booth, we looked toward the side of the store where it had stood; but there was no sign of a phone booth.

"Guess the phone company took it up when the store closed," noted Jubal.

We were standing there looking at the vacant spot where the phone booth had been when a small white panel truck drove up. The sign on the side said, "Councilman's Dairy Milk Delivered Fresh Daily." The image of a big black-and-white cow was painted under the lettering.

The man who emerged from the truck was dressed all in white with a white hard-billed cap to match. "Howdy, boys. Y'all lost or looking for something?" he asked.

"Looking for something," I answered. "Looking for the man who used to run this store: Mr. Godfrey."

"Well, you a mite late to find Mr. Godfrey here. Store ain't been opened since he went off to join the Army. You'll need to go back over toward Silas Creek Church to the cemetery there. He's been there since 'bout 1917. Got hisself killed during The Great War. Kind of a hero, I always heard when I was growing up."

Jubal and I were stunned. The Great War? World War I? How could that be? Just a couple of years ago we had talked to him. He had given us food and something to drink. We had gotten gas from that very pump that we were standing beside. To hear that he was a World War I hero, a dead war hero, was impossible for us to fathom.

"What kind of hero?" I stammered.

"Well, the way I heard it, was him and this other fella heard a baby cryin' in this church when they were defending this little village in France. They rushed into the church just about the time it blew up. When the medics went in after the battle ended, they found them two coverin' up the body of this little nigger boy who was still livin'. Come to find out, that boy had been in some kind of an orphanage run by some missionaries in the Congo, and they had hid in the church when the shellin' started. The missionaries had died in

229

the church too. The story goes that some descendant of some king or something took the boy and raised him. Don't know exactly what come of him, but that's the story far as I know it."

"Did he have any children?" I asked, thinking about the boy who had pumped the gasoline for us.

"Yeah, I believe he did. Seems like he had a son. I believe him and his mama moved back to her home after Mr. Godfrey got killed. Guess they figured they couldn't make a go of this old store by themselves."

"Nobody has run this store since World War I?"

"Nope. Old Man Jacobs had a produce stand here near 'bout every summer up 'til he died a couple of years ago, but the store's just been sittin' here gatherin' time."

Jubal and I just looked at each other. So many questions. *What had we seen here? Was this really the same place we had stopped at on our way home? Maybe there was another store further on down the road.*

"Is there any other store between here and Longview?" I asked.

"Longview? Don't know about any Longview around here. Back that way ain't nothing but paper-company land, miles and miles of young pine trees. Over that way you get on into the mountains pretty good, high country. If you keep on going past the dairy, you come to Martinsville; and if you turn off of the road, you go to Taggart. Where y'all from?"

"Taggart," I said reflexively. I was still so shaken by what the man had been telling us that I could hardly speak.

"Well, that's good. Y'all ought to be able to get back home before this storm comes up. Y'all be careful now." And with that, the milkman turned, got in his truck and drove away. I'm sure he had no idea of the impact his revelation had on us. We had come in search of the identity of the man who had sent the letter to Jubal.

Now, not only did we not know the letter-writer, we didn't know our own minds.

Chapter 27

On the way back to Taggart, Jubal and I went over and over the story the milkman had told us and tried to understand how his narrative reflected on our experience at the store a couple of years earlier. We determined that it was extremely unlikely that the whole experience had just been a figment of our imaginations because we recalled exactly the same things. We were close, but not that close. The afternoon experience was unsettling, to say the least.

As the milkman had recognized, there was a storm coming across the mountains. The thick, white summer clouds had turned almost black, and the wind had picked up. Green leaves were plummeting to the highway as the wind picked them prematurely from the trees and thrust them to the ground.

"Leon was with us!" exclaimed Jubal. "We've got to tell him about this. If he remembers the same thing we do, then it has to be real."

My concern for the weather and its effect on my driving disappeared as I pushed the gas pedal, increasing the speed of the car and sending us ahead of the threatening storm straight to the funeral home.

I drove the car under the portico of the mortuary just as the rain began to fall. Thunder sounded as we entered the foyer of the building and moved quickly toward Leon's office down the hallway. He wasn't there. We immediately went on down the hallway to Miss Hazel Merritt's office. Miss Hazel had been the secretary-receptionist-office manager at the funeral home for many years. Everybody in town knew to call Miss Hazel when they needed the services of the funeral home. She might not have been the president or even the owner, but she was the boss.

"Where's Leon?" blurted Jubal as we rushed into Miss Hazel's tiny office.

Miss Hazel looked up at us in her usual unruffled manner and asked calmly, "And how are you boys this afternoon? Looks like you have gotten here just in time to keep from getting wet. Leon has just been called out to a wreck downtown somewhere, over toward the bank, I think. He'll probably have to take somebody to the hospital from there so it'll probably be a while before he's back. Can I help you with anything?"

"No, ma'am," replied Jubal. "It's sort of a personal matter."

"Well, I'm sure he'll be glad to help," she said. "I just think it's wonderful that you have a father figure to turn to now that Leon and your mother are married. Leon is a fine man and a good example for you to follow."

"Yes, ma'am," responded Jubal. He was getting used to people telling him what a fine man his mother was marrying; and, as much as he agreed with them, he thought he had had enough assurance over the last few years that by then, folks could assume he knew the situation as well as they did.

But at that particular time, neither Jubal nor I wanted to wait for counsel from Leon. We wanted to talk to him right then. "Thank you, Miss Hazel.

I believe we'll just go on and try to catch him later," allowed Jubal as we turned and ran back toward the car parked under the portico.

As we exited onto the portico, the rain seemed to slack up a little bit; but it was still sufficient to make for hazardous driving conditions on the narrow streets of Taggart. I looked at the wet sky apprehensively as I started to get in the car. Most of the boys my age were much more confident in their driving ability. A few even had their own car. But I was limited to driving Dad's old Buick when I needed a car; and it wasn't a showcase for my driving skills, nor did it add to my image as a young man about town so my experience behind the wheel was limited.

"Come on, Raymond. Let's go. We'll meet Leon at the hospital," instructed Jubal.

"I've never driven in the rain," I said. "Dad'll have my hide if I wreck his car."

Jubal could tell I was a little hesitant. "Well, take it slow then. Just don't think on it too long. We need to get there before he leaves."

As I pulled out on to the street and eased the car toward the hospital, I remembered a fateful ride with Leon on a rainy day just a couple of years before. It had been part of an adventure story that we were still trying to unravel. I drove carefully. I wasn't ready for another adventure.

Chapter 28

The Taggart Memorial Hospital was not a very impressive building. It had only sixty beds, an emergency room for nonsurgical patients and one surgical room, all in one single-story building. But for a town the size of Taggart, is was a source of community pride. It was only about twenty years old and the only medical facility within the area. A doctor who chose to come to Taggart didn't come because he thought he could make a lot of money, but he knew he would be needed and could stay as long as he wanted.

I maneuvered the car into a parking space that was designated for emergency vehicles. I figured we met that description. I could see the hearse/ambulance backed up to the emergency-room entrance. The red light on top of the black vehicle was perched precariously at an angle, still blinking opaquely through the rain. Beside it was parked a police car, its light matching the one on the ambulance.

We walked quickly through the emergency entrance into a wide hallway with a receiving area on the right side just inside the door. The nurse behind the counter was dressed in the usual uniform of white with a starched cap.

"We need to find Leon McCoy, ma'am," said Jubal.

The nurse didn't even look up from her paperwork. "Just have a seat over there," she said. "He'll be back in a minute. He had to take a gunshot victim into the surgery room."

The nurse spoke with such authority that we didn't question her instructions or ask any questions. We sat down in two of the chairs among the five placed against the wall of the wide hallway.

"Gunshot victim?" asked Jubal. "I thought Miss Hazel said he had gone to a wreck."

"She said he had gone to the bank. I bet there was a robbery. That's how come the police car is here," I suggested.

It wasn't very long before we saw Leon coming down the hallway. He was pushing a gurney with bloody sheets piled on top.

"Hey, fellas. What y'all doing here?" he asked when he saw us waiting there.

"Somebody rob the bank?" I asked.

"Kinda. Fella came in the bank, asked for Mr. Vernon Seymour, walked over to his office and shot him with a shotgun. He's going to be alright, but the guy that shot him is as dead as a door nail. I got to go back and pick him up and take him to the funeral home."

"He's still lying dead at the bank?" I asked in amazement.

"Yep," he replied. "Unless he's come back to life, he's not going anywhere.

You have to know your priorities when you're the only ambulance in town."

"Who shot him?" asked Jubal.

"Oh, he wasn't shot. Don't know exactly what killed him; but best I can understand, as soon as he shot Mr. Seymour, the man doing the shooting fell over dead right there. Best guess without looking at him is that he had a heart attack. Probably have to get the coroner to determine exactly what killed him. Got to have an inquest and all that, you know. 'Course, you do know that John Dudley just got elected coroner, and he's not a doctor; he's a barber. So unless it's pretty obvious what killed him, we probably won't ever know. Dr. Lloyd told me he'd get me qualified, and Chief Gains said that with my experience being at just about every traumatic death in the county, I'd be sure to get elected; but that hasn't happened yet."

"The body can wait a little while longer then," said Jubal. "We got to talk to you about something real important."

"Well, I can't wait too long. I can't leave the man stretched out there in the lobby of the bank. 'Course, they closed the bank; but, still and all, I need to get on over there. Y'all ride with me. We can talk on the way."

When we went by the nurse's desk, I stopped to ask her if I could use her phone. She said it was for emergency use only, and I told her I had an emergency so she let me use it. I called Dad and told him that Jubal and I were going to ride with Leon back to the funeral home. Of course, he knew all about the bank shooting. His first response after he was assured we were alright was, "Get Leon's take on the story for the paper." He said for me to leave the car keys at the nurse's desk, and he'd send somebody over for the car. I'm sure he was as leery of me driving in the rain as I was.

On the way to the bank, Jubal and I filled Leon in on all that had transpired that afternoon back at Godfrey's Store. He was as dumbfounded as we were.

"I didn't imagine that," he said firmly. "I remember stopping at that store just as clear as if it were yesterday. I'm sure of it because, if you remember, we were about to run outta gas and that was the first and only place we saw where we could get it. And I remember the man in the store too and the sassy boy who pumped the gas. The milkman must have been pulling your leg."

The three of us went over and over our recollections of the stop at the store.

We all had exactly the same memories. We began to speculate as to why the milkman would make up such a story when he didn't even know us.

When we got to the bank, Jubal and I went over to the police officer who was standing guard at the door. "He still there?" asked Jubal.

The officer looked at Jubal as if he couldn't believe anybody would ask such a stupid question. "Unless he's Lazarus, he's still in there," replied the officer dryly.

We went to help Leon get the gurney out of the hearse/

ambulance and waited while the officer opened the door. The body was, indeed, still there. Somebody had placed him in repose. He was lying on his back with his arms folded across his chest. He wore an old brown suit, a white shirt with no tie, black shoes with white socks. Just an ordinary-looking man. But he wasn't ordinary. He was the milkman.

"Good god amighty!" shouted Jubal. "That's the milkman we just talked to this afternoon!"

"What?" asked Leon.

"This is him. This is the man we talked to, the one who was telling us about the man who owned the store and died in France.

This is the milkman," continued Jubal as we both stared in disbelief.

"Just calm down," said Leon. "It don't really matter who he is, I got to load him up and take him to the funeral home. You get his feet, Raymond, and help me put him on the gurney."

I did as Leon instructed. As we raised the man to the gurney, his arms fell to his side; and something came loose from his hands and fell to the floor. Jubal picked it up. It was a small rectangular piece of leather with a name stamped on it: "Leonidas J. Godfrey, Esq."

"That's the name of the man who sent me the letter," said Jubal. "Why does this man have his name? Wait a minute, wait a minute! I've got a card just like this one. Prince Albert gave it to me and told me to never lose it, and I still got it at home. I plumb forgot about it. When I got the letter, I never put the name together with the old piece of leather. It means that somehow Prince Albert and the milkman and the lawyer who sent the letter are all connected."

"Well, you keep thinking on all that as long as you want; but right now we got to get this body to the funeral home," said Leon.

So we helped Leon put the body of whoever the man was in the hearse/ambulance and took him to the funeral home.

Chapter 29

Two nights after we took the bank gunman to the funeral home, Jubal got a call from Leon, "Jubal, you need to come down to the funeral home right now. There's a man here says he needs to talk to you."

Jubal looked at the clock beside his bed and asked sleepily, "Right now? It's three o'clock in the morning."

"This can't wait 'til morning. The man has come to identify the body of the man from the bank shooting, and he said he needs to talk to you."

"Who is he?" asked Jubal.

"I don't know. He didn't tell me his name. He just said he could tell me who the man is, but you have to be here so get your butt down here right now." Then Leon hung up the phone.

The funeral home was three blocks from Jubal's house. He didn't have a car so he ran all the way. He ran in through the front door and down the hall to the back of the funeral home where the body of the man had lain since Leon had placed him there two days earlier. When he got to the room, he came to an abrupt halt. There before him beside the coffin stood Leon and a man that Jubal recognized immediately. He was dressed differently from the way

Jubal had last seen him, but there was no denying who he was. He had on a black suit, a blazingly white shirt and a solid red tie. The shine of his black shoes reflected the light from the floor lamp that stood beside him. Even in the soft glow of the parlor light, there was no mistaking the noble black face of Prince Albert Watkins. Gone were the old overalls and flannel shirt and slouchy felt hat that had covered his bald head. The man standing beside Leon looked like a man more accustomed to the sophistication of the city than to the simple solitude of an isolated cabin in the woods.

"Hello, Jubal," he said with a smile. "I must apologize to you and Mr. McCoy for arousing both you at this hour but I felt it necessary, given the circumstances."

Then he turned to Leon and said, "Mr. McCoy, this man is David Godfrey, my half-brother. If you inquire of the Register of Deeds office, you will find the statistical information you need to substantiate his identity. If you will take care of the burial of his body, I will pay you for your services, including the placement of an appropriate monument in the family cemetery."

"I'll be glad to, sir," replied Leon.

"Now, if you will, sir, I would like to speak with Jubal privately," said Prince Albert.

As Leon left the room, Prince Albert said, "Why don't we sit over here?" indicating two chairs placed in the corner of the room where the floor lamp stood between them. "Jubal, I fear that I owe you an explanation for so much of what has transpired since I last saw you. Preliminary to the explanation, I want you to know that I only wanted to help you without causing you any embarrassment or having to reveal to you any of what I am about to tell you. David's actions have caused me to present my story as an explanation, and I hope you will hear me out and reserve any judgment until I have told you all of it. Agreed?"

"Yes, sir," agreed Jubal, who was still stunned to see the man there.

"First of all, you must know that my real name is Leonidas J. Godfrey. I am the person who sent you the letter telling you of the availability of funds for your continuing education. I'll talk more of that later.

"My father was Jonathan Godfrey. He was a soldier in the American Expeditionary Forces sent to fight in France during The Great War. While there, he met a young woman who had become the ward of missionaries in the Congo. To phrase it delicately, they fell in love and, in a moment of ill-considered intimacy, produced a child: me. When the small village where we were living was attacked, my mother took shelter in the little church there, which subsequently came under fire from the Germans. My father and his friend rushed in to save us but were too late. They were all killed. I survived and was later adopted by an English family, the Watsons, hence the source of my name. I assumed that name although I have legally retained the name of my father to honor him and the fact that he sacrificed his life for mine.

"The Watsons were a wealthy family who provided well for me, and I appreciate them very much. They knew my father and told me many times of his heroism. Over the years I received a very good education, eventually coming to the United States to pursue a career as an attorney; and, upon the death of my adoptive parents, I inherited a great deal of money.

"I am very proud of my American heritage and was interested in pursuing the genealogy of my father's family. However, I discovered that the story of my father's death had been greatly modified to exclude any mention of my biological connection. In fact, I found that as his son, my ethnicity and his relationship with my mother would have been an embarrassment to his family so I never told them of my existence until a few weeks ago when I felt compelled to tell David, my only real biological connection to my father. David had never married, and I thought he might be glad to know that some part of the Godfrey family existed beyond himself. That was a mistake.

"To say that the news of the existence of his father's illegitimate nigger son was not well-received would be an understatement. Even when I offered, as evidence of my affection for my father and my appreciation for my heritage, to provide him a substantial income for the rest of his life, he remained irate, ranting that the knowledge of our relationship would shame the name of his family beyond any monetary value I might contribute. I told him I would assist him anonymously, but nothing I said could assuage his anger.

"In the course of trying to apprise him of how I could help him and his family, I told him about you and others like Jenny whom I would be assisting. I told him I had already sent a letter to the Bank of Taggart assuring your educational funding. He became even more irate, swearing that he would not let that happen. When you came out to the old store and he saw you there and realized who you were, he vowed then to prevent you from benefiting from my efforts. So, you know the rest. I guess he assumed that Mr. Seymour would be aware of my race and consequently feel compelled to tell everyone in Taggart. That was erroneous, of course, since Mr. Seymour and I had never met. Nonetheless, his actions have brought us to this point."

During the recitation of Albert's story—Albert was still his name, as far as Jubal was concerned—Jubal sat motionless, spellbound by the tale. When Albert had finished, there was a silence, a vacuum that seemed to suck the sense of reality out of Jubal's mind and memory. How much of what he had experienced was true? How much was real? How much was fantasy? If this man was not who he thought he was, how about all the other people he had met who were connected to him? Was Jenny real? Or Maybelle? Did his experience with those people really happen? How about the town of Longview? Who was the man that Leon and Raymond had spoken to at the old store?

Eventually Albert spoke again, "I'm sure that all I have told you here tonight is confusing, and I will not try now to clear away the cloud that fills your mind. Some things that you experience in life cannot be explained. Everything is not logical. When I leave here, we will not ever meet again; but I will always be a part of your life, as you will be a part of mine. Never doubt yourself, no matter how strained your spirit may be. Never question the credulity of the good in people, including yourself. Life is an adventure, a journey which you can never make alone, whether you choose companionship or not. Life is an endless dance in which you may change partners, but it is most important that you keep on dancing. We are all a part of each other." And with that, Leonidas J. Godfrey/Prince Albert Watson walked out of the funeral home. Jubal never saw him again.

Chapter 30

Prince Albert was right; he would always be a part of Jubal's life. The educational fund that he had set up at the Bank of Taggart was replaced upon Jubal's graduation from the university by a trust fund that would provide Jubal access to investment funds to begin his career. Jubal invested wisely and was largely responsible for the growth of his little town. He developed the first shopping center, built The Cavalier Hotel downtown and The Shenandoah Hotel and Resort over toward the Blue Ridge Mountains. Jubal served on the town council and helped bring the first community college to the area.

He built himself a nice house just a couple of blocks from Miss Jane and Leon. He could have afforded a great big house but said he didn't need a big house for just himself. It was a spacious ranchstyle brick house with a wide porch on the back that looked out toward the mountains. Jubal always said that if we looked hard enough, we might be able to see Longview from there.

Jubal led a happy and productive life. But he never got married.

Oh, he dated a few of the girls in town, even got real serious with Julie Canton over at the college one time; but he never seemed to find the girl he thought was just right for him. He and I talked a lot about Jenny. Of course, I never met Jenny; but Jubal talked about her so much I felt I knew her about as well as he did which, to tell the truth, wasn't very well. Every time we'd get into a conversation about his trip and Jenny, we'd both have more questions than answers. What kind of family did she come from? Was she living in Longview by herself? What happened to her musical career? We'd just speculate and make up stuff. One evening we were sitting out on his porch and Jubal asked, "You reckon I ought to try to find her, Raymond?"

"Well," I said, "you will probably never be satisfied 'til you try."

So he started sending letters to everybody he knew connected with the music business in places like New York and Miami and Los Angeles and Boston and Chicago, every music conservatory and performance venue he could find and any other place where he thought they might have heard of Jenny Balieu. He even flew to New York to ask the folks at Carnegie Hall and the Metropolitan Opera if they knew her. Nobody had ever heard of her.

One time we decided that we'd retrace our trip to Longview. That turned out to be a real disappointment. We went back to the old Godfrey store and headed back down the road that we thought would take us to Longview, but we never found anything that looked familiar. We looked on every kind of roadmap we could find, even got up with the folks who print the Atlas maps but never found a trace of a place called Longview.

One day Jubal got this idea that maybe Jenny was looking for him but didn't know where to look. So he decided he'd build a music venue right there in Taggart that would attract the biggest names in the music business. He went out to the Shenandoah Hotel and built a theater—I mean a state-of-the-art facility to seat a thousand people. He hired a fella he met at the Metropolitan Opera to run it. He got the university to set up an artist-in-residence program that would attract the biggest names in the business to come and stay there at the resort, and the music departments at colleges and universities from all over the South would send music students there in the summer. It was one of the finest programs of its kind anywhere in the world. His hope was that Jenny would hear about it and come there. She never came.

But one day he did get a call from some folks from an opera company. Well, not really an opera company, more like an *opry* company. The manager for a group called The Shanandoah Ramblers called and said they would like to come and perform at the theater. When Jonathan Marlowe, the theatre manager, called Jubal to ask if he thought it would be appropriate to have a bluegrass group perform on the stage at the resort, Jubal thought that it would certainly be appropriate. Bluegrass music was the music of his people, the people of southwest Virginia, the way he saw it; and when Jonathan told him it was The Shenandoah Ramblers making the request, everybody in Taggart could have heard Jubal shout.

I'm sure there has never been a more joyous reunion than the one with Jubal and Clement, Curtis, Craven and Melvin. The band arrived at the resort right after lunch, and Jubal met them there. There was a lot of hugging and laughter and some tears. They probably would have stood in the parking lot all afternoon if Jonathan had not told them they needed to get set up for the performance that night.

It was a memorable concert too. That theater was jammed with people from all over the area. When it was over, Jubal had the boys and me and a couple of other close friends go to his house. During the course of the evening's conversation, each member of the band brought Jubal up-to-date on the changes in their lives since Jubal had left them in front of the gas station in Longview. They had become very successful with recordings, awards and concert tours; and, if not wealthy, they were certainly prosperous.

"Remember," said Jubal, "I told y'all you were good. All you needed was a good business manager. 'Course, I thought it was going to be me."

"So did we," said Clement, "but that girl swept you off on the back of that horse; and we never heard from you again. Where you been?"

Where indeed? thought Jubal. He then proceeded to bring them up-to-date on his life without dwelling on the many obvious questions. He ended the night by offering to make the Shenandoah resort home base for the group. Clement said that sounded good, but they'd have to take it up with their manager. About a week later,

Jonathan got a call from a fellow named Reuben Long, the group's manager; and they worked out a deal in which the Ramblers played at the resort theater for a week every other month. It was always a sold-out performance.

The Ramblers continued to perform and record up until a few years ago. Melvin and Clement died shortly after their retirement, and Curtis and Craven still live at the resort... at no cost.

Before Clement died, he and Jubal tried to find Reverend Branson and Billy. They took off one morning and went over to Brimley Springs to see Clement's sister Myrtle. Clement had told Jubal that Myrtle had retired and was living in a rest home. He said he sent her money every month for them to take care of her, but he hadn't been to see her since she moved so this would be a good chance to see how she was doing and ask her about Reverend Branson.

Clement wasn't feeling well so he had Jubal drive his big bright-blue Lincoln over there. He told Jubal he really wanted a Cadillac like the one Hank Williams had but had decided that such a vehicle didn't project the kind of image he thought he needed. He never did explain exactly what that image was.

As they passed the sign that said "Brimley Springs," Clement said, "Myrtle closed up her café and service station, you know. After her husband died, she figured she couldn't run the service-station part. She tried to make a go of it with just the little café but told me that the population of Brimley Springs had shrunk to where she coulda fed the whole town three meals a day and wouldn't have made enough to pay the light bill. Think the man she sold it to tore it down and set up a car wash. Who'd ever thought there'd be a car wash in Brimley Springs? Turn here."

Jubal turned the Lincoln onto a narrow dirt road that passed through a stand of scrub pines and brush. At the end of the road were two small wooden buildings with a circular driveway and a small parking lot on the side. A small wooden sign in front of the bigger building read, "Brimley Springs Rest Home."

Jubal and Clement walked into the small lobby where a lady in a white nurse's uniform sat behind a metal desk. "Can I help you?" she asked.

"Yes, ma'am," replied Clement. "We're here to see Myrtle Ennis."

"And who are you?" she inquired.

"I'm her brother, Clement Todd, and this is our friend, Jubal Simpson."

"Well, y'all just take a seat over there on that settee, and I'll see if I can find her. Myrtle ain't always where she's supposed to be."

The lobby was sparsely-furnished with the one couch, a

straight-back wooden chair and a small lamp on a table beside the couch. On the wall was one painting of Jesus at the rock at Gethsemane and a framed copy of the license to operate a nursing facility in the State of Virginia.

In a few minutes the nurse returned and told us to follow her. "Myrtle's got a crowd down in the cafeteria singin'. She does that 'bout every day or so. It's near 'bout the only group activity we got going."

The cafeteria was a comparatively large room with about ten round tables with chairs. Myrtle was sitting on a short stool in the middle of the room with other folks, most of them in wheelchairs, sitting randomly about the room.

She had a guitar in her lap, but she was singing "You Gotta Walk That Lonesome Valley" a cappella.

You gotta walk that lonesome valley, You gotta walk it by yourself.
Nobody else can walk it for you.
You gotta walk it by yourself.

When Myrtle saw us, she stopped singing and said, "Now look what just walked in. Folks, this is my brother, Clement. Y'all probably seen him on The Grand Ole Opry. Now, he's got the talent in the family and I got the looks," she said with a laugh. "Come on up here, Clement, and sing something for these people."

Clement walked to where his sister was seated, gave her a hug and took the guitar. "Play something upbeat," she told him. "They need to be uplifted."

Clement took a few seconds to tune the guitar, then launched into "I'll Fly Away."

I'll fly away, O' Glory, I'll fly away
To a home on God's celestial shore,
I'll fly away…

Clement sang the old song with an enthusiasm that belied his age. That enthusiasm seemed to catch on with his audience as some of them began to clap to the time of the music.

When he finished to mild applause, Myrtle said, "That's the most movement I've seen out of some of these folks since I been here. Could be 'cause that's a real appropriate song for some of 'em. They purty near ready to fly away from this world."

Myrtle told the group that she'd be back later with some more music, then indicated for us to take a seat at the table beside her.

Clement said, "Myrtle, I thought you were in a better facility than this. I figured with the money you got from selling the café, your social security and what I been sending you, you'd be faring better than this."

"I'm doing fine," she said. "I decided to come here 'cause it looked like they could use some help with these folks. I didn't want to just go somewhere and sit and vegetate so I came to where I can do something for somebody else. Makes me feel good."

"Well, long as it makes you happy, it just tickles me to death," he said with a laugh. "I don't know if you remember my friend Jubal here," he said as he pointed to me in the chair beside him. "You remember the tent preacher who came to town and had the fire over towards Devlin's Store? He was with 'em."

"Oh, yeah," responded Myrtle. "I remember you and the preacher and that other boy. I tell you what now, that fire was the talk around here for a long while. Some folks thought the devil caused the fire since you boys was playin'. But turned out the Lord had his hand in it. Seems the preacher and Miss Cooper took up company and got married. They set 'em up a church over in the old hosiery mill on the other side of town. Done pretty good, I hear, 'til Miss Cooper died and the boy what come here with him come and got the preacher and took him off somewhere. I heard the boy was workin' for Oral Roberts. Don't tell that for the truth, but that's what I heard."

They talked a little while longer, then left Myrtle to resume what she called her *ministry*. Jubal reflected as they drove back to Taggart that Myrtle's ministry had actually started when she fed a wandering trio back so many years ago.

One day Rufus Cannon, the manager of the Cavalier Hotel, came into Jubal's office and told him they had to buy all new furniture for the hotel rooms. New government and hospitality association regulations said they had to provide no-smoking rooms. Seems that medical studies had proven that smoking was bad for your health and leftover smoke in a hotel room could cause cancer in the folks who slept there. So they spent all that money on new furniture and carpet at the hotel and at the resort. However, Rufus and Jubal decided to still keep some rooms for smokers. It was a matter of loyalty. After all, if it weren't for the tobacco farms in their part of Virginia, they wouldn't be there in the first place.

During the course of getting up-to-date on non-smoking regulations, Jubal was reminded of Maybelle Sykes and her tobacco farm. In all honesty Jubal had often thought about Maybelle as he continued his quest to find Jenny. The time they had spent at Maybelle's was a pivotal time in his life. It was at Maybelle's he had realized just how much Jenny meant to him, and it was there that he had lost her as well.

So, one Sunday morning he decided he would drive down to Minot Springs.

Since his previous arrival at Maybelle's had not been by the usual path, he decided to go to the town first. He figured the police station or the sheriff's office would be the logical place to start since they would know Marvin Lee.

He stopped at a service station just outside of town and got directions to the sheriff's office. When he got there, he went in the front door of the old brick building and told the officer at the desk he was looking for Deputy Marvin Lee Sykes.

"Don't believe we got anybody here by that name, sir," was the response.

"Well, he may be retired by now," continued Jubal. "I knew him and his mother, Maybelle, several years ago and just wanted to look them up."

"Oh, now, I knew Miss Maybelle. Everybody around Minot Springs knew Miss Maybelle Sykes. Fine woman. Tough, that's what she was. Tough as nails but good as gold. Ran that farm right by herself all those years right up 'til she died. That was 'bout ten years ago. Heart attack, I heard. Somebody said she just probably worked herself to death.

And I believe her son, Marvin Lee, did work here at one time. That was before I came to work here. I believe he got killed in a big wreck chasin' a car out in the country somewhere. Think he ran head-on into a tractor. Heard he was a good deputy."

"You wouldn't happen to know where Miss Maybelle's buried, would you?" asked Jubal.

"Sure do. Went to her funeral right there out at the farm. You can see it from the road. Little plot with a fence around it out in the field close to the house."

Jubal asked for directions to the farm and followed them through town and down the winding country road until he recognized the farmstead. It had changed considerably. The little road leading up to the house was barely visible, and the neatly-trimmed shrubbery around the building had grown so tall it almost concealed the building. The yard around it was covered in tall grass and weeds. The old barn had rotted, and what remained of it was leaning heavily. Where the old burned tobacco barn had stood was the replacement Miss Maybelle said she would build. It too was faded and leaning a little; weeds and vines climbed its walls, and the remainder of the tin roof flapped in the afternoon breeze. But it was there. She said she would rebuild and she did.

Jubal looked around at the abandoned fields, looking for the gravesite the deputy had told him was there; but he couldn't see it in such tall weeds. As he walked back toward his car, he glimpsed a tall bush standing above some weeds just a little way into the field beside the house. As he approached it, he could see at the top a gravestone and, as he got closer, the remnants of a wooden fence that had fallen around that monument and a smaller one beside it. He waded through the tall weeds until he stood before the marker and read the words inscribed on it:

Maybelle H. Sykes
Good Wife and Mother

The smaller tombstone read:

Marvin Lee Sykes
Son

Neither one had any dates on them. Whoever supplied the monuments probably didn't know when they had been born or when they died any more than he did... or Jenny.

As Jubal stood there at the little cemetery, his mind was filled with images of the time he and Jenny had spent with Maybelle. As the late afternoon breeze blew across the field, Jubal vowed to keep those memories. It seemed he could hear Maybelle's voice whisper to him, "You just get up and keep on goin'." Then he walked away and drove back to Taggart.

It wasn't long after Jubal got back from Minot Springs that Jonathan Marlowe, the theater manager, called Jubal and asked him to come out to the theater and look at some plans he had to update the stage and the sound system of the theater. They had been sitting on the couch and talking in Jonathan's office for a while when Jonathan got a telephone call. As Jonathan was talking on the phone, Jubal picked up a magazine from the coffee table. The name of the magazine was *The Chronicle of the Performing Arts,* and on the cover was a picture of an elderly lady and a young girl standing beside a piano on a stage. In small letters across the bottom of the page was a line that read: *One of Britain's Greatest Pianists Honored*. But Jubal did not see an elderly lady in the picture. He saw two young girls—one dressed in a beautiful velvet gown, the other dressed in a polka-dot dress just like she had worn sitting at a piano in a cabin in the woods. It was Jenny.

He hastily turned to the article in the magazine that told about the honor to be presented to Jennifer Watson. She was to become a Dame of the Most Excellent Order of the British Empire for her lifetime of work in providing piano instruction to the children of the Royal Family and "to those children placed in the orphanages throughout The United Kingdom." But the most exciting part of the story said, "The ceremony proclaiming Dame Watson a member of the order was held at Royal Albert Hall on 19 July. Dame Watson will leave immediately on a tour to promote pedagogy as a profession in the United Kingdom and The United States."

As soon as he finished reading the magazine article, he called me at the newspaper office. "Raymond, I've found her! She's in England! Meet me at my house in about an hour. We're going to London."

I didn't have to ask who he was talking about. Over the years Jenny had never been far from his thoughts. No matter what the occasion or event we became involved with, he would always say, "I bet Jenny would like this" or "I wish Jenny could see/hear this."

His thoughts of Jenny were not exactly an obsession, but they did occupy a lot of his mind.

By the time I got to his house, Jubal had gotten Jonathan Marlowe to call his connections in the music business to try and find out Dame Watson's itinerary. He was waiting for Jonathan to call him when I got to his house.

"She was in England, Raymond! We were looking for her here in this country; and we were looking for Jenny Balieu, not Jennifer Watson. It makes sense now if we think about it. Prince Albert's connections to the music world were in England. That's why he would send Jenny there."

The phone rang and it was Jonathan. "She's going to be at the Boston Conservatory of Music tomorrow night. I have arranged for you to get two tickets at the door. I also asked one of my friends there if he could arrange for you to speak with Dame Watson, and he said he would try to arrange it. Good luck."

"Wait," said Jubal. "See if you can find out where she's staying in Boston."

"Being a little optimistic, aren't you?" I asked. "Do you think she'll be willing to see you?"

"I don't know, but I'm sure going to try," he said.

I had not seen Jubal so excited in a long time. We rushed to the Taggart airport and talked Roy Duncan into flying us in his private plane to Boston. On the flight there, we speculated about what had happened with Jenny.

"No telling what kind of strings Prince Albert—or Leonidas Godfrey—pulled to make it all happen. She changed her name, became a British citizen. He must have gotten her some great instructors and put her in touch with the right people. You can't have better connections than the royal family," I said.

"Yeah, but Jenny made the most of his assistance. She knew what she wanted. Believe me, I know," Jubal said wistfully.

Jonathan wasn't able to find out which hotel Jenny was staying in so after we checked into our hotel, we called the theater and asked Jerry Olson, Jonathan's friend, if he had been able to send a request to Dame Watson for Jubal to see her.

"Oh, yes, sir!" he replied. "Dame Watson gave me a note for you that says she is looking forward to seeing you backstage tonight after the program."

Jubal was like a little boy in his excitement. "After all these years, she remembers me! Imagine that, Raymond. I'm a friend of a famous person!"

It never crossed his mind that he was a famous person, maybe not as well-known but famous for his philanthropy and his business acumen. The only person's opinion he cared about was Jenny's.

He walked excitedly around the room, then over to the window and looked out on the night sky as it settled over Boston. "Flowers! We've got to get her a whole bunch of flowers! Call the front desk and tell 'em we want two dozen roses, a dozen sent to the conservatory theater and a dozen for me to take with me."

The program at the conservatory was not to begin until eight o'clock, but Jubal couldn't wait that long so he called a cab and we left the hotel at about seven o'clock. When we got to the conservatory's concert hall, there were already people there. When we asked for our tickets, the boy also gave us the note from Jenny.

Jubal read it to me. "Jubal, so glad you are here. Meet me backstage after the program. Love, Jenny."

"Ha! She didn't sign it Dame Watson. She's still Jenny. Look, Raymond, it says, 'Love, Jenny.'"

It didn't take long for the concert hall to fill up with people as Jubal and I found our seats. They were in the back of the auditorium; but, considering the impromptu nature of our trip, we were lucky to get them.

A gentleman came out on the stage dressed in white tie and tails and proceeded to introduce Jenny. He pretty much followed the story that we had read in the magazine. He talked about what an inspiration Dame Watson had been to so many young people who had been able to express themselves through music. He read a long list of notable students who had gone on to become very successful in their profession. But I could tell that Jubal wasn't really listening.

He was on the edge of his seat, waiting for Jenny's appearance. When she did come out on stage, she was beautiful. Age had only enhanced her beauty.

The curtain opened behind her, revealing a full orchestra. Without a word, the elegant lady sat down at the piano and began to play.

"Rachmaninoff's Concerto Number Four," said Jubal as he turned to me. "I've heard her play it before."

The audience sat enraptured by the music as it swept over them. At the end of the performance, the applause was thunderous, shouts of "Bravo!" bounded across the hall and everyone was standing. Except Jubal.

I looked down at my friend who was still seated beside me. His eyes were closed, and his head tilted just a little to the side. He wasn't breathing. I knelt beside him and shook him but to no avail. My friend, Jubal Early Simpson, had died listening to music played by the person who had been the center of his life.

Epilogue

Jubal's funeral was a big event in Taggart. Everybody in town was there. People from all over Virginia were there: politicians, business leaders, some people who came just so they could tell people they had been at Jubal Simpson's funeral. I looked around at the crowd and was pleased to see such a diverse group. There were people from the entertainment business sitting beside college presidents, local farmers sitting with senators. They all came to pay their respects in their own way. I did know one older lady who came alone and sat on the back row of the church. Most people were dressed in black, but that lady wore a white skirt with blue polka-dots and white-and-black saddle oxfords. She didn't speak to anybody or say who she was. But I knew.

He had lived a long, productive and most interesting life. He influenced the lives of hundreds of people directly and indirectly and had changed his community. Everybody had their own stories to tell about Jubal.

After I spoke at the service, a lot of people told me that I should be the official biographer of Jubal Early Simpson. I agreed.

So, what I've done here is tell the story of his life as I observed it and just like he told it to me. I have tried to keep in mind his instructions to use the truth sparingly after all other resources have been exhausted.